The
Waiting

The Waiting

by
Hunter Shea

SILVER SHAMROCK
PUBLISHING

www.silvershamrockpublishing.com

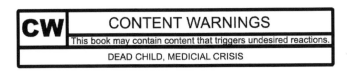

CONTENT WARNINGS

This book may contain content that triggers undesired reactions.

DEAD CHILD, MEDICIAL CRISIS

To the boy we left behind. I hope you've found peace.

FOREWORD

The year was 2014. I was still trying to crack my way into the horror writing business when I stumbled upon the work of Hunter Shea. I'd seen his name a few times on the Samhain Publishing website, but I hadn't yet read any of his books. Samhain's horror line published both novels *and* novellas, and it was one of those novellas written by Hunter that caught my attention and, after devouring it in one sitting, would make me a fan for life.

There are two amazing things to love about novellas. One, it's a quick way to discover new voices. And two, when done right, the pure joy and impact of a well-written novella can surpass even the best novels. There's zero room for filler. No wasted words mean you get pure heart and soul. You get characters, perfect pacing, and story— boom, boom, boom. Off the top of my head, I can name a number of novellas that stand shoulder to shoulder with plenty of my favorite novels: *A Dark Autumn* by Kristopher Rufty, *Darkness Rising* by Brian Moreland, *The Mist* by Stephen King. Newer novellas like *Crossroads* by Laurel Hightower and *True Crime* by Samantha Kolesnik continue the novellas compact and powerful tradition of literary perfection.

One of my favorite novellas of all-time is the one you're about to read, *The Waiting*. It remains my favorite piece of work by Hunter Shea. There's no cryptids. There's no death scene filled with blood and guts splattering across the page. There's no ghost hunters, no monsters, no devils. So what the hell is left? How about honest to goodness characters facing a horrible and unfair set of circumstances? Yeah, and Hunter punches us in the guts more than once in this story. As with his more recent release, *Creature*, this one feels extremely personal. The authenticity drips from the page convincing you you're now hooked to a machine that holds your life in the balance. You can't let go. Not until you understand just what in the hell is happening and you know it's safe.

The Waiting is a powerful tale of a newlywed couple that doesn't even manage to make it past their reception before tragedy strikes and places them in an agonizing situation filled with unanswered questions. We feel the frustration, the hurt, the anger, the weight of the mysterious illness afflicting this young couple and those closest to them. There's an all-encompassing sense of helplessness throughout much of this book that Hunter delivers as if he's suffering through it and fearlessly sharing that anguish with us as it happens. It's truly an amazing accomplishment.

And then of course, there's the boy. Is he really there? Are the characters so exhausted that their crumbling minds are messing with them? Or could he be something else? A ghost? Some misplaced spirit? If so, what does he want with them?

Hunter's prose has never been better as he leads us through this terrifying predicament one chapter at a time, each stroke of his pen scribbling us into increasingly darker shadows. The story pulls you in from the start and refuses to let you go until the final sentence. And in the end, you will be breathless. I guarantee it.

If you're already a fan of Hunter's, you know what lays beneath the guts, the gore, and the creature features. Heart. Tons of heart. And that's what makes this story, like many of the crazier ones in his catalog, hit so hard that you never forget. No matter how gentle the horror, *The Waiting* will leave a scar.

Glenn Rolfe
January 2021

BASED ON ACTUAL EVENTS

CHAPTER ONE

The pain lanced through Cassandra's stomach and bored its way down deep into her bowels. If she hadn't already had her appendix taken out when she was in high school, she would have sworn it had just burst like a cherry bomb. Her lungs convulsed and she drew in a long, ragged breath.

Keep walking, Cass. Just a few more pictures and you can sit for a while until everyone gets to the reception.

She felt someone grab her arm. Marybeth, her maid of honor and best friend, wiped the beads of sweat from Cassandra's forehead with her finger.

"You okay? You look a little pale," she said.

Marybeth reached into the bustline of her red satin gown and pulled out a handkerchief. She used it to dab the fresh spots of perspiration that had broken out across Cassandra's face.

"I'm fine," Cassandra said. "I think I have a little indigestion. I'll be all right."

Marybeth gave her a dubious look. "You haven't eaten in over 24 hours. You're probably starving. Or—"

Her bridesmaid, Andi, pulled up alongside her and whispered, "Or we got you and Brian before the priest just in time."

Marybeth and Andi chuckled, giddy from all the hoopla of their first wedding. Cassandra always seemed to be the first to take the big plunges. First to get a boyfriend. First to get a job—as a cashier at a dollar store. First to lose her virginity—to Sean Foster in the summer before her senior year. First to get engaged and the first one to get hitched in their small but tight circle.

And now she would be the first bride to throw up all over her expensive gown.

"Believe me, it's not that," Cassandra said. "I think it's nerves. I haven't been feeling right the past few weeks. I just want to get through tonight so I can relax on our honeymoon."

She smiled, and that seemed to be enough to take their minds off her pain.

"Andi, can you please find Brian and the boys so we can take these last pictures?"

Everything was forgotten when Brian turned the corner. He looked so handsome in his black tux and rose tie. His thick brown hair was held in place with just enough gel to last through a long day. His cobalt eyes fixed on her, and she could see their future in them.

God, I'm lucky, she thought.

She'd never once doubted her decision to marry Brian; never had an instant of cold feet. It was just all the other craziness that went with a big Italian wedding that must have given her an ulcer.

Brian pulled her close and kissed her softly on the lips. He whispered in her ear, "Honey, I know you look amazing in that dress, but I can't wait to get you out of it tonight." He nibbled her earlobe. It made her forget the fire that had erupted in her stomach.

"You better be patient, because this is not an easy dress to get off."

"We'll see about that."

He laced his arm around her waist and kissed the top of her head.

"Okay everyone, line up by the fountain out back," Preston, the world's most irritating photographer, blurted. He wore coke bottle glasses and had a waxed mustache that curled at the ends.

The reception hall was on a rise overlooking the Hudson River. The striated cliffs of the Palisades on the Jersey side of the Hudson provided the perfect backdrop for their wedding party photos.

"We better do what Salvador Dali says," Brian said.

Everyone laughed. It had been a rough couple of hours, being ordered into ridiculous poses when all they wanted to do was dance and drink and celebrate.

Preston shook his head at them, his hands on his hips, and walked off in a huff.

Brian led Cassandra off the dance floor and back to their positions of honor at the dais. They watched his groomsman, David, try to do "the worm" and almost take out a couple of Cassandra's older aunts in the process.

"Someone should really cut him off," Brian joked.

"Look at Aunt Jean's face," Cassandra said, laughing until tears came to her eyes. "Remember not to invite them to Sunday dinner at the same time."

"You know, back in college, Dave was the king of the dance floor."

She looked at him with disbelief. He couldn't keep a straight face. They broke out in a fresh round of laughter.

"I'm so glad you're not a good liar," she said, pulling him in for a kiss. His lips tasted like wine.

"And I'm glad I have you. In fact, I'm so happy I have the most beautiful bride in the world that I'm willing to sign you up to a ten-year deal right off the bat."

Cassandra pinched his cheek. "Sweet. Ten years, huh?"

Growing up, Brian had been a baseball phenom. Right after college, he was picked up by the Cincinnati Reds and worked his way through their farm system. She stayed with him through several small towns, a baseball wife-to-be. He was a left-handed pitcher with a rubber arm that could hurl a wicked curveball that brought lefties to their knees.

Then one day, the rubber snapped, and that was that. No more games. No more traveling on buses to tiny baseball towns. He may not have been able to play it like he once did, but the game was in his blood. He got a job as a high school coach and they were able to settle back home in the Bronx and reunite with their families. He never regretted a thing and didn't complain.

Brian liked to equate the stages of their relationship in baseball terms. It was their private joke.

"What do I have to do to get an extension?" she asked.

"Well, naturally, you have an opt-out clause around the seventh year. I think they call that the Itch Clause, but I'd advise against using it. At that time, we can renegotiate. You play your cards right, we can get you another multi-year deal."

She kissed him again. After seven years, he still made her heart flutter.

The sound of silverware clanging against glass egged them on to kiss a little longer, and that was fine by her.

The DJ faded the music out and announced, "Ladies and gentlemen, please take your seats while the happy couple, Mr. and Mrs. Brian Pagano, cut their wedding cake."

"Come on, babe," Cassandra said, pulling him off the dais. "And promise you won't smash it all over my face."

Brian only smiled. That could mean anything.

The four-tiered cake was on a table that was wheeled over to them by a pair of waiters. Between each layer was a ring of red and pink edible roses. The table was decorated with real rose petals. The DJ played "The Bride Cuts the Cake" and everyone clapped along.

Brian placed his hand over hers, and they made the first slice. It was put on a plate for them and they were each given a fork.

"Remember, you want to see me out of this dress tonight," Cassandra said, grinning.

"Oh, I do," Brian said. He gingerly placed a small forkful of cake in her mouth. As she chewed, he swiped a dollop of icing on his finger and plopped it on her nose.

"See, that wasn't so bad," he said.

Everyone applauded and laughed.

"Now it's my turn," she said. She gathered a heaping portion onto the fork.

Brian's eyes lit up, and he opened his mouth as wide as it would go.

Their families and friends cheered her on.

The pain in her abdomen came on like a gunshot. The fork fell from her hand, and she collapsed on the floor.

The burning agony was so intense, she couldn't draw a breath, couldn't even cry out in pain.

Something just exploded inside me! Brian, please help me!

Cassandra pulled her knees toward her stomach, but nothing could stop the relentless crashing waves of torment. A sickening heat flooded through her, and she started to go numb. She heard the startled cries of everyone in the reception hall. Brian cradled her head in his lap and brushed his hands across her face.

"She can't breathe," he shouted.

Cassandra felt pressure on her neck. It was too hard to make out the shapes of the throng of people that had gathered around her. Their faces blurred. Their voices echoed in the deepening distance.

Her stomach pulled into a tight knot, and she felt hot bile rocket up her throat.

She thought she was crying.
And then even thought was robbed from her.

CHAPTER TWO

"Mr. Pagano?"

The surgeon, Dr. Patel, entered the waiting room with tired eyes and slumped shoulders.

Brian's heart stopped. He tried to swallow, but it felt like his throat had closed off. Alice Torre, his mother-in-law of seventy-plus hours, gripped his arm as they rose from their chairs.

The surgery was supposed to take two hours, three tops. At least that's what they had been told ten hours earlier. Other families had come and gone during that span, leaving with relieved smiles. Brian and Alice were the only ones left.

"Is...is she okay?" Brian stammered. His mouth had trouble forming the words, each one thick as molasses.

Dr. Patel placed a hand on his shoulder. "She's in recovery. I want to keep her sedated for now."

Brian's head spun and for a moment, he thought he was going to fall back into the chair. He felt his muscles release the tension that had been building since the moment Cassandra had passed out at the reception. He had to bite his lip to hold back a wave of tears.

Alice asked, "What happened to her? Why did it take so long? Is she going to be all right?"

The doctor motioned for them to take a seat.

"I'll be honest with you," he said, "we didn't expect to find the massive amount of damage to her bowel system that we did. At first, I thought it was an intestinal blockage, which *was* part of the problem. Was she complaining of abdominal pains before the wedding?"

Brian shook his head. It was hard to concentrate on everything the doctor was saying. He'd never felt this drained before.

"She did mention a stomach ache a few times over the past month, but I just assumed it was nerves. And she was starving herself to fit in the dress. Did that have something to do with it?" Alice asked. She pulled her hands into her lap and pressed her thumbs together until the tips were white.

"I can assure you, a pre-wedding diet wasn't the cause. When I went in to target the area where we had located the blockage, I found gangrenous abscesses throughout her entire digestive system. We had to remove her lower intestines to find the root of the problem. Her ileum, which is located at the very bottom of the lower intestines, had ruptured. It must have happened some time ago for gangrene to set in."

The word *gangrene* brought Brian out of his torpor. He leaned closer to Dr. Patel.

"How is it possible to have gangrene and still be able to walk around? I thought people only got that from infections when they were wounded," Brian said.

Dr. Patel stroked the white hairs of his short, trimmed beard. "When Cassandra's ileum burst, it leaked toxins into her digestive tract. Those poisons ate away at the tissue, turned gangrenous and caused multiple perforations of her intestines. The pain she was feeling must have been extreme. We had to remove a good portion of them, along with part of her stomach. I had to insert multiple drains that will have to remain in place for the next few months to ensure all of the poison has been evacuated."

Brian felt Alice's arm rest across his shoulders.

"What concerned me was why her ileum ruptured in the first place. Then I remembered her chart and saw that she had been taking anti-inflammatory medication for a period of several years."

"Yes," Brian said. "She used to take them for the pain flare-ups in her shoulders and hips."

The doctor nodded. "For the Ehlers-Danlos, I understand. Her condition is very rare and I'm afraid no one has the answers on how to best cope with it. At the time, anti-inflammatories were the best answer. Now we know that they can weaken the soft tissue of the gastrointestinal tract, which is why we don't prescribe them for long-term use."

"When can we see her?" Alice asked.

"I'll let you look in on her once we move her to ICU. I'm afraid she may be here for some time. This was a very big surgery, and recovery is going to be slow and painful. She's very, very lucky to be alive."

Brian fixated on the words *slow and painful*. His teeth ground together, sending spikes of pain into his temples.

Why didn't you tell me, Cass? Was it because you thought it would ruin the wedding? Why couldn't you share your pain with me? What I wouldn't give to take your place in that recovery room.

A flood of impotent rage swept through his body. He was mad at fate, God, even himself for letting this happen to his wife.

Brian didn't notice Dr. Patel leave the room. Alice touched his cheek and brought him out of the fury of his emotions.

"Come on, let's get a soda downstairs and some air," she said. "Maybe in an hour or so they'll move her up. It'll do us both good to see her face. Then we can go home and get some sleep."

A long exhalation deflated Brian's anger and he nodded. "Sure. I feel like I could sleep for days."

But sleep didn't come easy when he lay on the couch of his apartment after midnight. He kept seeing her pallid face with tubes running in her nose and mouth, surrounded by machines. They hadn't allowed him to go in the room. He wanted so badly to kiss her, to feel her warm hand in his, to tell her that he loved her and for her to fight.

He stared at the boxes scattered around the living room, wondering when he'd be able to unpack them in his and Cassandra's new home.

"We should be on our honeymoon now," he said to the darkened room.

Brian watched the shadows move across the ceiling as the night dissolved into day, waiting for visiting hours to begin.

CHAPTER THREE

Because Cassandra was young by the hospital staff's reckoning, they had put her in a colorfully painted private room in the pediatric section after several weeks in ICU. Visitors had packed every corner of the room with flowers, teddy bears, balloons, and get-well cards. Brian brought fresh yellow carnations, her favorite, every three days and kept them by her bed.

Her moments of lucidity were few and far between. When she did wake up, the pain would burn like a bonfire in her eyes and he would call for the nurse. She was given high-dose injections of Dilaudid, and her eyelids would flutter before she fell back into a narcotized sleep.

Cassandra hadn't spoken a word since the surgery. At first, they were concerned there may have been brain damage. The infection had poisoned her blood and tissue and there was a chance some of it made it to her brain. A battery of tests proved her brain was functioning normally.

"She *will* talk," Dr. Patel had reassured him. "When it's time, she'll talk. Until then, you must talk to her, let her know you're here. Your combined will can do more than I can at this stage."

Brian was reading Cassandra's favorite book aloud, *The Outsiders*, when there was a light knock at the door.

Marybeth came in carrying a big plastic bag.

"How's the patient?" she asked, setting the bag on the lone empty spot of the windowsill.

"No change," Brian answered, placing a bookmark between the pages. He hugged Marybeth and watched her place a soft kiss on Cassandra's cheek.

"I brought you something for lunch and dinner. Take out from Romano's. You look like you haven't been eating, so I got a little of everything. Promise me you won't let this go to waste."

Brian smiled. "I promise. Actually, I am kind of hungry."

She reached in the bag and handed him a foil-covered wedge. "Good. Have a veal and pepper parm. You need to keep up your strength."

The sandwich was this side of Heaven. He didn't remember eating the first half before the second half was almost devoured. Wiping his mouth with a napkin, he looked at Cassandra, at the tubes running in and out of her chest and stomach, and was sick with guilt.

Here I am making a pig of myself and Cass hasn't put solid food in her mouth for over two months.

Marybeth saw the look on his face and rubbed his shoulders. "I know, Brian. It's not easy. You're doing everything you can. If Cassandra could talk, she'd tell you she was proud of you and so happy to have your love. You know that, right?"

"Yes. I just feel so helpless. I come here every day, stay here until visiting hours are over, and nothing changes. It's like we're in limbo, and I don't know how to get us the hell out."

He rubbed Cassandra's hand, wishing with every fiber of his being that she'd magically wake up.

It was a long day with visitors coming and going. Saturdays were always the hardest. Brian did his best to keep a brave face and assure friends and family members that she was progressing and would be well soon. He wondered if he said it to console those who loved and cared for Cassandra or to convince himself that there was more hope than he was feeling.

Most likely it was both.

The PA announced that visiting hours would be ending in fifteen minutes. Brian tucked the blanket around Cassandra and smoothed the hair from her face. He inspected the drains and IVs to make sure everything was in place. He couldn't leave without knowing that everything was as it should be.

He turned when he heard someone walk in the room.

"Dr. Stepka. Making the late rounds?" he said.

Cassandra's primary physician had been her doctor since she was seven and had told Brian on more than one occasion that he considered her more than a patient. She was like a granddaughter to him. Dr. Stepka was a broad man with a wide boxer's nose and thick yet delicate hands. His graying hair was in need of a trim.

"I was home, eating one of those prepared meals from the supermarket when I got the urge to come here. How has she been today? Any improvement?"

Brian shook his head. "Nothing. She woke up around three, but it didn't last long."

Dr. Stepka sat on the edge of her bed and consulted her chart. Both men were quiet, lost in their frustration and grief.

Brian was putting away the things he'd brought with him—a newspaper, a Jack Ketchum paperback, a pile of forms he had to complete for his insurance company—when he heard the doctor quietly sobbing.

"I'm sorry, Brian. Please, forgive me. There are nights I can't sleep, wondering what more I can do, who else I can bring in. As a doctor, you learn early on that you can't cure everyone. You try and try, but sometimes fate takes matters into its own hands."

He pushed his glasses atop his forehead and wiped his tears with the back of his hand.

Brian didn't know what to say. Watching Dr. Stepka break down was more than he could handle. He stood opposite the doctor, numb.

Does he know she's going to die? he thought. *How long do I have left with her?*

"Cassandra's strong," Dr. Stepka said. "She's always been a tough kid. That's what will bring her back."

"I know," Brian replied. It was a struggle to speak past a whisper. He felt his own tears building, but he refused to let them come. If Cassandra could hear him, he wanted her to know he was strong, that he wasn't giving in to despair. He had to feed his strength into her, just like the machines fed nutrients and medicine into her body.

The doctor placed a fatherly hand on her blanketed leg and composed himself.

An idea had been circling around Brian's brain for the past couple of weeks. He figured now was as good a time as any to broach the subject.

"I want to take her home," he blurted. "To our house, the one we picked out together. I want to get her out of this hospital. If she's going to get better anywhere, it has to be there."

Dr. Stepka sighed, and their gazes locked for what seemed hours, though could only have been seconds.

He nodded. "I think you should. She belongs with you, in your home. All we're doing here is providing a bed and changing IV bags. Yes, at this point, I think that's best. She'll need nursing care and someone to be with her 24 hours a day."

Brian's body felt limp with relief.

"I'll take care of everything," he said. He wasn't sure how, but he'd damn sure move heaven and earth to make it happen.

The doctor rose and shook his hand. "I don't doubt that for a second. *Save our girl*, Brian. I know you can do it."

CHAPTER FOUR

Brian pulled his car behind the ambulette and was waiting outside the rear double doors before the attendants came out. Fall had come early and crisp leaves whirled around the street in tiny eddies.

Cassandra's stretcher was removed with little fuss and great care. She hadn't stirred since they had prepped her for the journey home.

The single, two-story detached house they had bought four months earlier sat on a small plot of land in the Woodlawn section of the Bronx. The front yard was ringed with azalea bushes that had been a beautiful pink and purple when they had put their bid on the house. The cold air and diminishing sun had dulled their vibrancy.

Brian opened the door and said, "Would you mind if I wheeled her inside? It's kind of my one chance to carry her over the threshold for the first time."

"Yeah, sure," the burly driver said, stepping aside so Brian could take his place.

Quite a few windows in the surrounding houses sported parted curtains. Brian was sure this was the spectacle of the day. They would be the talk of the neighborhood.

He wheeled Cassandra through the living room, past the kitchen and into the back bedroom they had planned to make a guest room. The master bedroom was upstairs, but he wanted her down here in case there was an emergency and she needed to be taken to the hospital.

His footsteps echoed across the walls. Every room was littered with unopened boxes and plastic storage containers. The carpets had been a disaster, so he'd ripped them all up with his friend Mickey's help last Sunday. Ordering new carpets was somewhere on his massive to-do list.

The attendants wheeled Cassandra's life support machines behind her. They helped Brian transfer her to the hospital bed he had purchased and checked to make sure the IV tubes were clear and untangled and the port in her chest was connected.

"The nurse will be here in just a few minutes," the driver said. "She'll show you everything you need to do."

"Thank you." Brian said.

The men left and the house fell into a deep silence. He still had to get furniture for the place. His sole priority had been Cassandra. The back bedroom had her dresser and night table and Hello Kitty lamp she'd had since she was a kid. His bed was a blow-up mattress that was still in a box by her dresser.

The bell rang ten minutes later. An attractive, petite Indian woman extended her hand when he opened the door.

"Hello, I'm Louisa Gupta. I'll be your wife's home nurse."

Her smile gave him an odd sort of comfort and he led her inside. "My name's Brian. Cassandra's doctor said you have a lot to show me."

She had a black messenger bag over her shoulder that she removed along with her jacket. She looked for a surface to place them and Brian said, "As you can see, I have a lot of work to do. We were supposed to nest, that's what Cass called it, together. We'd gotten as far as picking out paint when, well, when she got sick."

Louisa shivered and put her jacket back on. She smiled again. "Believe me, I understand. If you're smart, you'll wait until she's better before you decorate. Now, where is our patient?"

Brian motioned to the back of the house. "Right down there. Would you like a drink? I have bottled water and bottled water."

Louisa removed two clear bags that were filled with a thick, milky fluid. "I'm fine, thank you. Would you mind putting one of these in your refrigerator? This will be tomorrow's supply. We'll use the other one now so I can show you how to hook it up."

When they entered the bedroom, Brian noticed Cassandra had turned onto her side in her sleep. She had rarely moved in the hospital. He prayed it was a sign that he had done the right thing in bringing her home.

"Help me move her onto her back," Louisa said. Her voice was soft, gentle, as light as her touch as she guided his wife into a better position. "It's best to keep her this way so she doesn't lean onto the drains. The last thing we want is for the tubes to pinch and stop the flow."

Brian pulled a small notepad out of his back pocket and wrote it down. "I'm ready to learn," he said, waving the pad.

"Good." The nurse looked at Cassandra's pale, placid face. "She's a very beautiful woman. Between the two of us, we'll get her back on her feet."

The calm confidence the nurse exuded was infectious. For the first time in months, Brian's chest felt lighter. The crushing weight of impending tragedy had been lessened by several pounds.

"Now, let's clean out the port in her chest," Louisa said.

Thunk.

The noise came from the room above their heads. It was followed by two smaller, shuffling sounds. Louisa paused, holding the collar of Cassandra's gown.

"Something must have fallen. I've kind of thrown everything around the house. I haven't had time to unpack most of our stuff."

She nodded, but a cloud of doubt flashed behind her eyes. It was gone before he could comment.

Louisa said, "Tonight, you watch me. When I come back tomorrow, I'll help you do it." She pulled the wrapping from a fresh needle and punctured it into a tiny bottle. "This is heparin. I use this to clean the port and keep your veins nice and clear. After this, I'll attach fresh tubing into the IV bag and thread it into the infusion pump. It's very important that you make sure there's no air in any of the lines."

Brian watched her every move, scribbled what she said as fast as he could. Now he knew what laser focus meant.

It took all of ten minutes, and when she was done, she asked, "Are you certified for CPR?"

He ran his hand through his hair and said, "Back when I was a lifeguard in high school. It's been a while."

She placed her bag onto the kitchen counter. "I'll review the basics with you, but it's also a good idea to take the course. The more you know, the more in control you'll feel."

When she left fifteen minutes later, he had to admit he felt like he had a better handle on things. He was still terrified of the thought of being in charge of Cassandra's life support, but like baseball, practice would make perfect.

Only in this case, one strike was all he was allowed.

He watched Louisa's car pull out of the driveway. The steady, whirring drone of the infusion pump kept him company while he looked for the air pump for his bed.

CHAPTER FIVE

The doorbell rang, pulling Brian from a deep, dreamless sleep. The air mattress protested with cranky groans as he maneuvered himself onto the floor. He touched Cassandra's hand with his fingertips in passing and jogged to the door.

Alice Torre stood on the doorstep, surrounded by matching maroon Samsonite luggage.

"How's my favorite MIL?" he asked, kissing her on the cheek and grabbing her bags. "You sure you haven't left anything behind? How the heck did you get these out of the car?"

"You forget I used to work in a bakery. Twenty years of lugging sacks of flour and sugar make you strong."

Brian asked, "Do you want me to show you your room, or do you want to see Cassandra first?"

She pointed down the hallway. "I can hear her machine. I think I'll let her know I'm here."

He concentrated on the larger bag and said, "I'll bring everything upstairs for you."

Her heels clacked on the bare floor. He heard her talk to Cassandra with the same joy and enthusiasm as she would if her daughter were well and able to greet her back. It was comforting. The house had been so quiet the past couple of days.

"Please don't tell me you're sleeping on an air bed," Alice said when he joined her at Cassandra's bedside.

"Just for now. I pretty much spent our furniture money on her hospital bed. It was more than my first car. I can assure you, I have a bed for you upstairs."

She placed her hands on his cheeks. "I'll buy you a bed. You have room for a single in here."

"I'm fine. Save your money for the party we're going to throw when Cassandra gets better."

Alice sat by Cassandra's side and ran her fingers through her daughter's long, silky hair. "My baby. Now you have your husband and your mom."

Brian said, "I can't thank you enough for moving in. If I don't get back to work, I could lose my job, and if I lose my insurance, I don't know what to do."

She kissed the tip of Cassandra's nose and moved off the bed. "There's no thanking your new MIL. Since her dad passed away, living alone hasn't been a bed of roses. If I can't take care of my kids, and that means you, too, what else can I do? I'll be here until she gets well or you kick me out."

He laughed. For a moment, he thought he should give her a hug, but then he pulled back, not sure what to do. He was still learning the ropes of dealing with a mother-in-law.

She pulled a silver rosary from her pocket and placed it on the rolling IV pole that held the pump. "Every little bit helps," she said, running her finger down the beads.

"Come on, I'll show you the upstairs, then make you the best dinner you've had in weeks."

Alice arched an eyebrow. "You're going to cook?"

"No, but I know a place that delivers amazing Cuban food."

As they walked up the stairs, Alice noted how loud their footsteps sounded. "Where are the carpets?"

"At the dump. Trust me, they probably had more diseases in them than the labs at the Center for Disease Control. I'll get some installed soon."

"At least put something on the walls. This place is an echo chamber."

But that's what Cassandra couldn't wait to do, he almost said.

It could wait, everything could wait, until she got up from that bed.

After dinner, Cassandra's nurse came to the house to watch how Brian handled the life support machine. Alice liked the nurse right off the bat. What a sweet girl. And she was doubly impressed by her son-in-law, or SIL as she liked to call him, as he connected a fresh bag of the nutrients that kept Cassandra alive and installed the tubing in the pump and her daughter's chest like he'd been doing it for years. His hands did shake a bit when he flicked the hose to make sure all of the air bubbles were out.

The nurse, Louisa, said it would be her turn next time around. If she was going to be here to take care of Cassandra, she'd have to learn. She wasn't sure she could be as brave and secure as Brian, though. She still saw Cassandra as the little girl who used to fall asleep on her lap while they watched Barney. It would be hard injecting life support into her baby.

After Louisa left, Alice said, "I think I'll go to my room, settle in and read a bit. I get up early, so you might as well sleep in on your last day before work. I promise I'll be quiet when I check on Cassie."

"Thanks. See you in the morning, MIL." Brian tied up a black garbage bag and headed for the back door.

"Good night, SIL."

Alice went up the stairs, the wood creaking and protesting with each step. *At least no one can sneak around this house. No need for a burglar alarm*, she thought.

She opened her handbag and took out the two books she wanted to get a few pages into before hitting the light. The first was a Tess Gerritsen mystery. That girl could write. The second was her constant companion, the Bible. They all needed the Lord's help right about now. Brian wasn't a churchgoer, so she would just have to double her efforts to bring Cassie back from the brink.

The Bible went on her nightstand and the mystery on her pillow.

She took a hot shower and changed. Brian had ordered a bed and dresser for her and said it had been delivered just the day before. The wood smelled fresh, new, and the surface shined. It took a while to move everything from her suitcases to the drawers and closet, and when she was finished, she was good and exhausted.

After stowing her suitcases in the back of the closet, she went to settle into bed. Slippers were kicked off, and she said a silent prayer as she sat on the edge of her bed.

"Amen," she whispered, making the sign of the cross.

As she turned to pick up the mystery book, she pulled back, confused.

"I could have sworn I put it on the pillow," she muttered.

The Bible was still on the night table, alongside a digital clock.

"Where on earth?" She got out of bed and walked around the room. Maybe it had fallen while she was putting things away. The space under the bed was empty.

Determined, she checked the bathroom, then the dresser.

She found it tucked away in her shirt drawer.

Another example of old timer's disease. Alice chuckled. She settled back into bed and read until her eyes were too heavy to stay open.

CHAPTER SIX

The first day back at work was difficult. Everyone had been warm and sympathetic. Even the kids went out of their way to welcome Brian back and ask how his wife was doing.

It was hard to concentrate. Running the kids through warm-ups, he thought of Cassandra.

Getting the JV baseball team into the weight room so they could build up some muscle in the off-season, he thought of Cassandra.

Even during lunch in the teacher's lounge, with Mark Runde talking about his sky diving trip that weekend—he was feeling the bite of middle age and fighting back—he thought of Cassandra.

By the end of the day, for the first time since he'd started working in the school, he resented it. The sight of the sprawling building, the pencil lead and bleach smell of the hallways, the cacophony of a thousand teens shuffling to their classes, all added to a growing grudge against a world that made him have to come to this place just so he could keep his wife alive.

He should be with her, not here pretending everything was okay and that he cared whether Tommy Sapeda did all of his required push-ups.

He knew today wasn't going to be easy. He didn't anticipate such anger.

It's not the school's fault and don't take it out on the kids. Cassandra is in good hands. You'll see her soon.

The bell rang for seventh period and he forced a smile as a swarm of sophomores streamed into the gym.

Alice found a box marked *dishes* and set about washing them and putting them in the kitchen cabinets. She did the same with the glasses and coffee cups. She sensed that if she left it up to Brian, they would have stayed in those boxes until Cassie got up to do it herself.

It wasn't that he was lazy. He was in a holding pattern.

She didn't blame him one ounce.

Cassie snored in the next room, and she went in to check on her. Her mouth hung open slightly and one hand was balled into a fist. Alice stroked her hair.

"Are you having a nightmare, honey?"

At her touch, Cassandra's fingers relaxed. Her eyelids fluttered and for a moment, it looked like she was about to wake up. These were the moments she and Brian both looked forward to and dreaded. To see Cassie's warm brown eyes, to connect with her, was a blessing.

But those precious moments never lasted long. The pain would bully its way through and Cassie's mind would retreat into the numbness of sleep. Sometimes, when the pain was so bad that tears streamed down her face, her mouth still unable to work, they would put a morphine patch on her arm. It didn't take long for that to take effect, and Cassie would fade away.

Alice waited until Cassandra settled, and her breathing was more regular and calmer.

Needing to straighten things up, to feel useful, she tripped on Brian's mattress and almost fell into the pole holding the life support machine.

She straightened herself an inch before colliding with it. "Thank you, Jesus, for holding up a clumsy woman," she said, her eyes heavenward.

Her nerves jangled, she said, "You should have seen that one, Cassie. I know how much you like to laugh when I stumble around. Think I'll get the paper and see how much better we have it than the rest of the world."

The *New York Post* was wrapped in a plastic bag and sat on the lawn, a good twenty feet short of the porch. It was a nice day, the sky a pale blue with the occasional pulled sugar puff of clouds. The air was crisp, cleaner now that the smog of summer had passed and the sunlight seemed sharper. Fall in New York was her favorite time of year.

As she bent to pick up the paper, she noticed an older woman on her small porch next door. She sat on a white resin chair, holding a needlepoint within a small, wood circle.

"Good morning," Alice said.

The woman worked the needle in one side, pulling it back out the other. She took no notice of her.

Must be hard of hearing, Alice thought.

She looked at Cassie and Brian's house. It *was* pretty, with new light brown shingles, decent size front and backyards, a covered porch—a rarity in the Bronx—and plenty of room for a growing family inside. How she prayed they would one day provide her with lots of grandkids.

A movement in the upstairs master bedroom window caught her

attention.

The white lace curtains she had hung up earlier parted, then wafted against one another as if someone had been peeking out and ducked away from the window.

That was odd.

It couldn't have been the wind because all of the upstairs windows were closed. It had been chilly last night and she shut them all sometime around midnight.

Alice couldn't tear her gaze from the window. What was she waiting for? To see if Cassie had miraculously gotten out of bed, climbed the stairs, and was spying on her?

"Maybe it's a ghost," she said, laughing to drown out the sudden sense of unease that washed over her.

A garbage truck rumbled by and broke the spell.

It was just a draft. The house, though renovated, was old. Bound to be gaps in the windows where a breeze could filter through.

She looked down at the paper in her hand, forgetting that it was the reason she was outside in the first place. Tucking it under her arm, she went back into the house. The old lady next door never once looked her way.

CHAPTER SEVEN

"You want to stay up and watch a movie?" Brian asked Alice. He'd been back to work for a full week now and was in desperate need of something to take his mind off his negative feelings toward the school.

Alice pushed the dishwasher door shut and turned it on. It started with a deep rumble and a hiss of spraying water.

"I think I'll take a rain check. Louisa had me do the hyperal hook-up today and my nerves have been shot ever since. I don't know how you stay so calm."

He wasn't sure either. There were theories that men could compartmentalize things easier. Emotions went in one box while action was pulled from another. It was either that or he had missed his calling as a home nurse.

"It's all about practice," he answered. "You'll see. A week from now you'll be just as good as me or even Louisa."

"I don't know about that." She pulled a dishtowel from her shoulder and plopped it on the draining board. "But I do know that a bath is calling. See you tomorrow, kiddo."

She came over to the couch where he was resting with his feet up on the recliner and kissed the top of his head.

"I'm going to look for carpets tomorrow," he said.

"Good. These floors are so slippery, you'll be taking care of me and my broken hip in the bed next to Cassie."

He heard every step as she walked to her room, then the bathroom. The faucets squealed as they turned and water splashed into the tub.

Brian plucked the remote from between the couch cushions and looked for something funny to watch on all of their streaming services None of the new stuff looked the least bit appealing. He searched for older movies and smiled when the highlighted cursor found *The Big Lebowski*.

"The Dude abides," he said, and clicked OK to watch his favorite movie.

Alice had gone to bed and the Dude was having Donnie's ashes blown back into his face when Brian heard a slow creak. The sound bounced around the walls of the hallway leading to his and Cassandra's bedroom.

He paused the movie and looked down the hall.

Creeeaaak.

A sliver of light slashed across the floor and lower part of the wall.

The light grew brighter as their bedroom door swung open. The handle bumped into the wall with a dull thud.

Cassandra!

If she was up, her legs wouldn't be able to hold her weight for long. Brian stumbled off the couch and ran to get her. His socks skated across the floor and he slid into the bedroom.

Cassandra lay still, the pump humming away, pulsing with the milky fluid that fed her.

She hadn't so much as moved a muscle since the last time he'd checked on her.

Brian looked at the wide-open door. A disconcerting tickle danced across his lower back.

Old uneven doors.

He shivered, and decided to call it a night.

CHAPTER EIGHT

Marybeth and Brian's friend Tony came to visit one night. He asked them to stay for dinner and Alice whipped up a fettuccine carbonara that was out of this world. Tony dove in for his third helping.

"Mrs. Torre, you mind coming to live with me?" he said.

"If I did, you wouldn't be long for this planet," she replied, laughing. "Brian said you had a big appetite. God bless. Eat up."

Marybeth had excused herself to go to the restroom. When she returned to the kitchen, she said, "I couldn't help myself. I had to check on Cass again. Her color looks better."

"Has she been able to talk at all?" Tony asked.

"Not a word—yet," Brian said. He finished his glass of wine. "The doctor said she will. All of the moving parts are fine. It's a form of mutism brought on by trauma. When she can be awake for longer periods of time without the pain, she'll talk."

What he didn't say was how a small piece of him died every time he looked into her eyes and saw the hurt. He did everything he could to keep her comfortable. If only she could tell him what she was experiencing, maybe he'd find a better way to make it disappear. It was a fantasy, thinking that he could banish her pain through the magic of her voice. But fantasies and hopes were all he had to go on.

Marybeth and Tony stayed for a while longer, until she checked the clock on the kitchen wall and said, "Oh jeez, I better get home. I have a report that needs to be done before I get in the office tomorrow. I just love spreadsheets."

Tony rose from his chair and stretched his arms. "I better hit the dusty, too. Mickey's off, so I have to open the shop. A morning person, I'm not. Though I will sleep good tonight, thanks to Momma Torre." He rubbed his belly.

Brian shook his head. Tony was a master of lightening up the mood of a room. A dose of Tony was just what he needed. His anger had been simmering for weeks now. He was angry at the doctors for not getting Cassandra well. Angry at the insurance companies that expected him to decipher the mounds of paperwork they sent daily. Angry at work for taking him away from Cassandra.

He'd told Alice about his growing rage one night. She'd assured him it was natural. Anyone would be mad in his position. Life demanded to go on, but the most significant part of his life was being held back. He was relieved when she told him she often felt helpless and downright pissed at times.

Marybeth went into the living room, then came back to the kitchen. "Okay, where did I put my keys?"

"I thought you left them on the coffee table, sweetie," Alice said.

"Yeah, me too," Marybeth replied, still searching.

"Well, there aren't a lot of places where they can be," Tony said. "Brian's still got a lot of furniture to buy and stuff to unpack." He clapped him on the shoulder.

Brian said, "Maybe you brought them with you when you sat with Cassandra. I'll check."

It didn't take long to see the keys were not in the bedroom. Marybeth, Tony, and Alice were in the living room looking around the boxes and containers.

"Any luck?" Brian asked.

"Nope," Marybeth said, frustrated. "And this is my spare set. I lost my other set a month ago at the mall."

Tony shouted, "Bingo." He twirled her key ring on his finger and tossed it to her.

"Where did you find them?" she asked.

He shook his head. "In the last place you'd look. They were up here, on the windowsill."

Tony stood beneath the high-set window above the couch. It was made from colored glass and was a decorative addition to the house. The colors were too deep to see through, but it made nice patterns in the room when the sun shined through it.

"How the hell did they get up there?" Alice asked.

"I know I didn't put them there," Marybeth said. "I couldn't even reach if I wanted to. Tony, are you messing with me?"

She slapped his arm with the back of her hand. He winced.

"It wasn't me," he protested.

"Right." She hugged Alice and Brian. "Thank you so much for dinner. Cass really looks better. I can feel that it'll be any day now."

"Thanks. I hope so," Brian said.

She sneered at Tony with mock contempt. "And *you*, I'll see you around."

He held up his hands in surrender. "I swear, I didn't put them there."

Brian heard them quibble as they walked to their cars.

He looked over and saw the old lady next door, ensconced in her chair. He and Alice had made several attempts to talk to her but were always met with blank stares. Several times a week, a younger person came to check on her; must have been one of those companion services. The Meals on Wheels people brought her dinner every night.

For the first time since he'd moved in, she looked at him with something close to open, yet silent, communication. Her lips parted as if to say something, but she sneezed instead. Her head gave a slow nod, and she trained her gaze back on the street-lit block. Marybeth and Tony pulled their cars away. The old lady continued nodding.

CHAPTER NINE

"MIL, have you seen my iPod?" Brian called up the stairs.

Alice's head appeared over the banister. "I wouldn't even know what an iPod looks like. Is it big, small…?"

Brian rechecked the pockets of his jogging jacket. Empty. He always kept his iPod in his pocket. Running was the only time he had to listen to music.

"Never mind," he said. "I'll look for it later."

He went to the bedroom to make sure Cassandra's life support machine was working. Earlier, he had been woken up by the chiming of an alarm. The fluid had stopped moving within the tubing as it should and he had to open the pump's door and rethread the IV tube. That had been two hours ago, and he kept waiting for the alarm to sound again.

"I'm going out for a run," he said. Cassandra lay fast asleep, but he kept hoping she could hear every word he said. He kissed her dry lips and headed out the back door.

The missing iPod bothered him the entire time as he wound his way down the neighborhood side streets, coming to Indian Field. He liked to run within the trees of the park. It was his version of bipedal off-roading. The air was thick with the sweet smell of pine needles.

He had over a thousand songs on his iPod. And like a moron, he'd never bothered to back up the audio files.

Gotta find it.

He pushed himself, doubling his pace so he could get back home and renew the search.

Rain lashed against the windowpanes, and Alice caught brief glimpses of the dark clouds bustling through the night sky between lightning bursts. She hated storms; had since she was a little girl. Her father used to tell her it was just God letting off some steam. That scared her even more.

There was a soft knock on the door.

"Come in."

Brian walked in wearing his Reds jersey and baggy sweatpants. She called it his *staying home uniform.*

"Can we talk for just a sec?" he asked.

"Yeah, sure." Alice shifted in the chair, and he motioned for her to stay.

"Look, I can't tell you how much I appreciate your coming here and helping take care of Cassandra. If it wasn't for you, I'd never have been able to bring her home."

"I told you, you don't have to thank me."

He held up a hand. "*And*, I'm especially thankful that you've put the house together with the little bit I've brought over. If it was just me here, this place would be a disaster. That being said, I think we need to set up some rules about moving my things."

"Is it the iPod thingy again?"

He'd made such a fuss searching for it the other day. Even furniture was turned upside down in his hunt. She was the one who found it, sitting in the flatware drawer, when she was making dinner.

Brian had a lot on his plate, and she tried to explain that he was bound to forget things, to do stuff out of his normal routine. It was a miracle he remembered to put on pants every morning.

"No, that's where it should be, or at least it was last time I checked," he said. "I'd just appreciate it if when you see my stuff around the house, you leave it there."

"Honey, you have to help me out here. What stuff are you talking about?"

He sighed and leaned against the door. Thunder rumbled.

"I had a clipped pile of insurance forms that have to be in the mail tomorrow. I know they looked like a mess, but I was planning on going through all of them tonight. Please don't tell me you threw them away."

Alice knew she had to choose her words carefully. He was being polite, but she could see and even feel the anger stirring just below the surface. Brian was always happy, outgoing, the loudest in any group. Lately, she'd noticed a big change. Sure, since the wedding, he'd been somber, distraught, stressed to the max, but his kindness and humor were always present.

Since going back to work, he'd been quiet, moody. He hadn't blown up yet, but she could see it would happen soon.

"I know what you're talking about. They were on your dresser and I knew to leave them alone. In fact, I saw them there about an hour ago when I went to give Cassie a sponge bath."

Brian rolled his neck until it cracked and he flexed his fingers, balling them into tight fists. "Shit. If I don't get them done, I could be hit with a ten-thousand-dollar bill that'll take months for the reimbursement. And I don't have ten grand in my account."

Alice rose from her seat, dropping her Bible on the bed. "Come on, I'll help you look."

"I'll find them. Sorry I bothered you." He turned away before she could respond and ran down the stairs.

She stood in her doorway, listening to him grumble and curse as he stormed throughout the house. Multiple shards of lightning lit up the room. Strange, unfamiliar shadows leapt onto the walls and in that brief moment, she thought she saw a small, dark shape dart across the hall. It had happened so fast, she couldn't be sure what it exactly was that sprang to life in the flicker of a lightning bolt.

Alice closed the door. She didn't want to be able to see into the hallway.

It was irrational, downright silly. But something about that imagined shadow startled her, and no amount of rationalization would make her open that door.

CHAPTER TEN

Alice woke up the next day to a quiet house. The storm had passed and Brian had left for work. She put on her slippers and padded down to Cassie's room. To her surprise, she was awake. Cassie's eyes moved from the ceiling to her.

"Good morning, baby. Mom's here." She stroked her cheeks in light brushes with the back of her fingers.

Her heart melted when she saw the recognition in her daughter's eyes. They looked around the room, settling on the infusion pump.

"That's your breakfast, lunch, and dinner," Alice said, smiling. "You can't believe how great Brian is handling it. I'm still a nervous mess. I worry so much about hurting you."

Cassandra tried to move her hand. It shook at first, and she was able to raise it an inch off the bed. Alice scooped it into her own.

Thank you, God! Alice reveled. This was the first time Cassie had been so aware, had even tried to move without it being something she did in her sleep. Alice tried to fight back tears, but it was a losing battle.

Like her daughter, words escaped her. They dove into one another's eyes, saying a million words between each blink of their lashes.

Then Cassie's gaze drifted to someplace just over her shoulder. Her eyes widened and her lips pulled into a tight line.

"Honey, what's wrong? There's nothing to be scared of."

Alice turned her head but only saw the dresser beside the window. *Ding-ding-ding-ding-ding!*

Every alarm went off on the life support machine at once.

Brian ran into the house, breathless. Since Alice's frantic call to his cell, he'd sprinted from the school, leaving third period gym class without supervision. He broke every traffic law on the books driving home and twice almost rear-ended the car in front of him. His heart fluttered like the blades of a weather vane in a hurricane.

"What's wrong?" he shouted.

Alice sat on the bed holding Cassandra's hand. "I don't know." The infusion pump whined and screeched. "She was awake and coherent, and then the alarms came on. I didn't know what to do. I called Louisa, too."

Brian looked at the machine, saw that it had stopped. Something must be wrong with the line. He clicked the latch and removed the cover, unwound the tubing. There were air bubbles everywhere.

"Hold this," he said, handing a section of the IV tube to Alice.

He pulled out a pair of latex gloves from the box by the bed and put them on. Then he lifted Cassandra's shirt until he could see where it connected to the port by her chest. He placed his fingers on the metal ring just below the surface of her skin and pulled the needle free from the short tube with his other hand.

Then he filled a small syringe with heparin, swabbed everything down with alcohol, and flushed out the port. People connected to hyperal were at high risk of infection and he could leave nothing to chance.

When he was done, his legs gave out and he collapsed into the chair he kept by the bed.

Cassandra had been unconscious during the whole ordeal.

"If it wasn't for the warning systems in that machine, she'd be gone," he said, his voice an octave above a whisper. He brought Cass's hand to his mouth and kissed it. Alice stood at the foot of the bed, silent, stunned.

Louisa came five minutes later and double checked the machine, IV line, and bag. When she was sure everything was fine, she reconnected it and cleaned the drains from Cassandra's stomach.

"She'll be okay," Louisa said. "Sometimes this happens. You did the right thing, Brian." She placed a reassuring hand on his upper arm. Her jet black hair was pulled in a ponytail and her almond eyes glimmered with pride.

Brian smiled, but inside, he wanted to scream.

CHAPTER ELEVEN

There hadn't been a repeat of Cassandra's lucid moment in over a week. In fact, she had gotten worse. She was running a temperature, and a second IV bag, this one loaded with antibiotics, had to be hooked up each day to hold off whatever infection was raging in her body.

Louisa had told Brian the ports inevitably had to be removed because of infection every six months or more. It might be time to take this one out and move it to the other side of her chest. The scars would be far from minimal, but he knew Cass would look at them as a good thing when she pulled out of this.

If she pulled out.

Brian was supposed to get a physical for work but he'd been putting it off because he knew his blood pressure would be off the charts. He felt like an overfilled water balloon most of the time. The strain was reaching new heights, but he had to keep his shit together.

Cassandra came first, and he had to be there for her. But there was so much other crap to do. He hadn't even looked for the carpets yet and he was in hot water with the principal for leaving the school without telling anyone. And then there were the bills, insurance forms, calls from doctors.

Tony had suggested he join one of those boxing gyms to help relieve the tension. Somehow, he knew punching a speed bag wouldn't quite cut it. This stress had to be cut down from within, and he wasn't sure how to do that until his wife got better.

He was sitting at the kitchen table when Alice jarred him from his private misery party.

"I'm going to the book store. I need to restock. You need anything while I'm out?" She buttoned her fall coat and pulled her hair out from under the collar with her fingers.

"If they have one of those miracle cures, you can pick one up for me." He tried to sound casual, but the crinkling of her eyes told him he failed. They locked in a brief stare-down. He wasn't about to have his bluff called. Building walls had become his latest expertise. At this rate, he'd be a master in a month.

Alice broke first. "Trust me, if that existed, I would have bought it long ago. I'll be back in a couple of hours."

He made a meatloaf and mashed potatoes so he'd have leftovers for the next few days. Money was getting tighter than a violin string and he couldn't afford to buy lunch every day. The act of cooking, then cleaning, helped to take his mind off things. It was all very Zen, losing yourself in the mundane motions of everyday tasks.

While scrubbing the meatloaf pan with a wire brush, he decided he'd move the TV into the bedroom tonight and put on Cass's favorite movie, *Blithe Spirit*. She loved old movies. Maybe that would help the healing process.

As he was putting the last of the pans in the cupboard, he heard a sharp crack in the hallway.

It sounded as if something heavy had leaned on the old wood flooring.

He thought, *That's not the house settling. That was way too loud.*

Brian froze, still bent at the waist, his hand in the cupboard, afraid to drop the pot in its place and mask any follow-up sounds.

Crick.

That was much softer, like the ticking of the roof when the chill of night set into the old house.

Tiny beads of sweat broke out along his hairline.

What the hell am I afraid of?

"This is ridiculous," he said, dropping the pot on the shelf with a loud clang. He pulled the dishtowel off his shoulder and tossed it over the back of a chair.

Anything to delay the joy of untangling the wires behind the TV, he kidded himself.

Two steps out of the kitchen, he looked down the hallway and stopped.

Who is that?

A small boy stood in the center of the hall.

He looked to be about eight or nine, with crew-cut brown hair and small, green eyes. The boy wore a heavy, blue sweater and tan corduroy pants. He stared at Brian, and Brian back at him.

Neither spoke.

Neither moved.

The boy's face was expressionless. It was as if he were wearing a mask, and a damn good one at that.

Brian looked back at the front door to see if it was open. Maybe the kid had wandered inside. He didn't want to scare him.

"Hey," Brian said. "I didn't hear you come in. You startled me. Do you live around here?"

The boy stared back, silent. Brian realized the kid hadn't even blinked. Was he in some kind of shock?

"My name's Brian. What's yours?"

The shadows in the hallway grew darker, the light from the kitchen and the bedroom dimming ever so slightly.

Still the boy didn't move, didn't speak.

Brian took a small step toward him and the floorboard popped.

The boy spun around and ran into the bedroom.

"Wait, don't go in there!" Brian shouted. He pictured the scared boy slamming into the life support and pulling everything out of

Cassandra in the process.

As he followed the boy, a frightening thought flittered across his brain.

How is that kid running and not making a sound?

Every step in the house brought groans of protest from the aging wood. Yet, somehow this strange boy could dart across the floor as if he were two inches off the ground.

Brian made it to the bedroom and gasped.

The boy wasn't there. Cassandra lay propped up in bed, her cheeks rosy with fever.

He checked under the bed, then the closet.

There was no sign of the boy and no exit other than the window, which was closed with the latch still in place.

Brian's head spun.

What the fuck just happened? Where did that kid go?

He looked in every corner of the house and came up empty. He returned to the hallway, standing in the exact spot where the boy had been.

Brian bent over, clasping his knees and breathing heavy.

"I'm losing my mind."

CHAPTER TWELVE

Louisa was happy to accept the offer of coffee after checking on Cassandra. She had tried to get Alice to work the tubing into the pump, but her fingers were too unsteady, too uncertain. Some people could never get comfortable with the process. Louisa didn't blame them. You held the life of someone you loved dearly in your hands, and one wrong move could be fatal. She marveled at people like Brian who mastered it in no time.

"How do you like your coffee?" Alice called from the kitchen.

"Milk, two sugars," she replied.

She packed her things into her messenger bag after putting the spent needles into the red hazardous materials bin. The only thing missing was her pen, a gold Cross pen her father had bought her when she graduated nursing school. She looked at the night table, then within Cassandra's rumpled sheets.

The long, cream window curtain caught her eye. It billowed out as if there had been a sudden gust of wind. She could see through the diaphanous material that the window was closed.

A chill raced through her. She shook it off, looked down, and found her pen sitting on the floor between her feet.

Odd. That had been the first place she'd looked.

Louisa looked around the room, searching for what, she couldn't say.

She couldn't shake the feeling that someone was watching her. She glanced down at Cassandra, but her beautiful patient's eyes were closed in quiet repose.

Collecting her things, Louisa pulled the blanket up to Cassandra's neck and walked to the kitchen.

Alice had laid out a platter of cookies, crackers, and scones. A package of sweet Irish butter was nestled in the center of the plate.

"I wasn't sure what you liked, so I threw a little bit of everything on there," Alice said.

"I see," she said. "I don't think I'll leave here hungry."

She had coffee and talked with Alice for half an hour, assuring her it wasn't a failure that she wasn't comfortable with the life support machine yet.

All the while, a tremor of concern built deep in her gut. She couldn't keep herself from stealing glances down the hallway, into Cassandra's room.

Brian's stomach woke him up in the middle of the night. He'd barely eaten dinner, hadn't been eating much at all lately, but he was tied up in knots like he had spent the night downing White Castle belly bombers. Clutching his stomach, he pulled himself up from the air mattress by gripping the end of Cassandra's bed. He gave the infusion pump a quick check before walking with halting steps into the bathroom.

The house was still, in direct contrast to Brian's mind. The incident with the boy, now several days in the rearview mirror, had him questioning his sanity. *Better to let it go, chalk it up to stress*, he'd been telling himself.

There was a sharp click, followed by amber light that crept within the gap between the bottom of the door and the frame.

Brian was just finishing up. *Guess I made more noise than I thought.*

"Sorry, I didn't mean to wake you, mom" he said.

Alice had been doing so much, caring for both him and Cass, that she had to be just as stressed as he was. She needed her sleep, not him bumbling around.

There was no reply.

Alice had her own bathroom upstairs, so she was most likely in the kitchen grabbing a drink or a small bite to eat. The thought of eating made Brian nauseous. But he could use a glass of water.

He opened the door and flinched.

The boy was back in the hallway, staring at the bedroom.

An icy, numbing sensation spread from Brian's core to his extremities.

No. He can't be there!

Brian blinked hard and gripped the doorknob. If he reached out, he could touch the boy's shoulder. That's all he needed to do to confirm that he wasn't losing his mind; that the boy was physically in the house.

All it required was a simple moment of brief contact.

But he couldn't bring himself to do it. A terror as rich and real as his boyhood fear of prowlers breaking into the house at night kept him rooted to the spot. He wanted to speak, to say anything to get the boy's attention. His vocal cords were frozen, locked into shocked silence.

The boy never once looked his way, never wavered from his concentration on the bedroom seven feet away. Brian listened to the soft whirr of the life support machine, could even hear Cassandra's light exhalations.

Do something!

It was the boy who moved first. Without a sound, he proceeded down the hall and into the bedroom. Brian watched him stop at Cassandra's bedside. He tilted his head to be closer to her face.

The boy's lips moved but even in the silence, Brian couldn't hear a single vowel, much less a word.

What is he saying to her?

The boy straightened, his eyes never leaving Cassandra.

A soft, small voice began to sing, but the boy's lips never moved.

Oh hush thee my baby,
Thy sire was a knight.
Thy mother a lady,
Both lovely and bright.
The woods and the glens from
The towers which we see,
They are all belonging,
Dear baby to thee.

The melodious, disembodied voice made Brian's heart palpitate. It flowed from somewhere in his bedroom. The boy swayed like tall grass in a soft breeze as the lullaby was sung.

The voice grew softer and softer until it hushed out of existence.

His paralysis broke. Brian's feet touched the cold wood of the hallway floor and he walked toward the bedroom, weaving like a sailor on leave. His vision spun, then pulled into long, wavy lines like taffy. He watched the boy whisper to his wife.

One step from the bedroom, the boy's head snapped to face him. It only lasted a moment, and Brian saw nothing in his eyes but an emptiness as vast and unknowable as the depths of Europa's mysterious seas.

Brian cringed when the boy straightened and ran past him. He pulled back, colliding with the wall, his fear of coming in contact with this…this…phantom overriding any natural impulses to grab the pint-sized interloper by the collar and demand to know why he was in his house.

When he turned to see where the boy was running to, he was gone.

Brian felt his legs give way, and he slowly inched downward until he was sitting on the bedroom threshold.

What's happening to me? He bit the soft flesh of his palm to keep from screaming.

Who the hell is that boy? Why do I keep seeing him?

He stayed there the rest of the night, in the space between the hall and the bedroom, watching, waiting, worrying.

Real or imagined, he vowed to keep the two incidents to himself. No one could know.

No one.

CHAPTER THIRTEEN

Alice waited in her room until she heard Brian close the door and his car pull out of the driveway. His mood had taken an even darker, more secretive tone over the past few days. Her attempts at bringing him into a conversation were met with grunts or monosyllabic replies. Since moving the TV into the bedroom, he was rarely in any other part of the house, other than the kitchen to eat and the bathroom.

That he was playing all of Cassie's favorite films each night helped relieve some of her worry. *He doesn't need to talk to me, or even be polite. He has to be with Cassie and help get her through this.*

Despite their efforts and the attention of Louisa and the doctors, Cassandra was getting worse. Her waking moments were happening less and less. Alice's dreams were plagued by thoughts of the morning when they had connected as Cassie's way of saying goodbye.

Alice worried constantly about her daughter, but it wasn't until recently that she considered there might come a day when she would lose her. When she had first arrived at the house, she could feel the hope that crackled in the air. Like all energy, it had come and gone, morphing into something new, in some*place* new.

Now the house felt cold and expectant. Her negative thoughts weren't helping the situation. All of Cassie's pain and their worry were building a cocoon of despair. Somehow, they had to find a way to break free of it.

Well, today she would try her best to dispel the negativity.

Cassie was going to come out of it. Things always get worse before they get better.

She knew Brian never left the house without making sure all of Cassie's machines were pumping and draining away. That meant there was time for a shower before heading downstairs. Better to start clean and new.

When she was done, she wrapped a towel around her hair, put on a nice shirt and jeans, and walked down the noisy stairs.

"Good boy," she said when she saw the half-full coffee pot on the warmer. Brian made it a little weak for her taste, but beggars can't be choosers.

Alice had bought a handful of gossip magazines at the bookstore. She wanted to make today a silly girl day, even if Cassandra couldn't laugh or groan along with her. Then maybe she'd take a cue from Brian and pop in a movie and watch it with her.

As she walked out of the kitchen, she said, "Cassie, honey, you're never going to believe who Brad Pitt is fooling around with."

The mug slipped from her hand, bathing the floor and her feet with piping hot coffee. If there was pain, her mind was too stunned to register it.

A small boy sat at the end of Cassandra's bed. One knee was bent and most of that leg was on the comforter. The other was locked straight, his foot flat on the floor. He looked at Cassie with beautiful, shining eyes and a round face with skin as flawless and smooth as fresh cream.

He didn't look away, despite the crashing of the coffee mug and her sharp gasp of surprise.

The sun filtered through the window. It bathed him in a diffusion of soft, yellow light.

Alice's heart raced and her hands trembled. She found it hard to keep her grip on the tabloids.

The boy moved with surprising grace, shifting off the bed and seeming to glide to the head of Cassandra's bed. He bent forward, and Alice lost sight of him for a moment. When he straightened, he smiled, then reached out to the control panel of the infusion pump.

Part of her wanted to yell at him not to touch it. If she thought a real, living boy was in the room with her daughter, she would have.

But she knew what she was seeing was not an actual boy.

The certainty of what she beheld kept her mouth from opening and her legs from propelling her into the room.

She watched him turn his back and walk around the bed until he disappeared from view within the doorframe. She was struck by how quiet the house was. The boy's footsteps didn't elicit a single tick from the cranky wood floor.

When he was gone, the infusion pump started to howl. It broke her trance and she walked over shards of ceramic, leaving coffee and crimson-colored footprints in her wake. She was not surprised to see the boy had disappeared.

She *was* concerned about the warning chime on the pump. When she looked down, the floor by the bed was covered in a foul-smelling miasma of blood and clots of infected tissue. The drain tube in Cassandra's stomach had slipped out. Her digestive acids must have flared up, spewing rot and gore from the open wound the surgeon had left.

The smell was overpowering. She clamped a hand over her mouth to keep from vomiting.

What do I do?

Her finger shook as she jabbed at the monitor, trying to turn off the alarm. When she moved closer to inspect the vitals display, her foot slipped in the vile essence of the infection that was taking Cassandra from her and she fell backward.

She looked up at her daughter, who wore an expression of absolute peace.

Still on the floor, she fumbled for her phone and called Louisa.

CHAPTER FOURTEEN

This time, when Brian got the call from Alice, he kept his calm. Louisa was there with her and would wait until he got home. He assigned Noel Rice to be the gym monitor while he jogged to Principal Mann's office.

Knowing Louisa was already there, calm and in control, made the biggest difference this time around. He drove fast, but didn't blow past stop signs and red lights.

Alice was on her knees cleaning something off the hall floor.

"Is she okay?" he asked, pausing before going into his and Cassie's bedroom.

"Yes. I kind of panicked, but it's a good thing I did. Louisa can explain it better than me."

He saw bandages on her feet but concern for Cassandra was overriding.

Louisa rose from the chair by the bed and motioned for him to join her. The veins in his head pounded and he had to take a deep breath to collect himself.

The first thing he saw was the tilted lid of the medical waste bucket. It was stuffed with paper towels and rubber gloves spattered with blood.

"Oh my God, what happened?"

Louisa said, "It was nothing critical. Please, take a seat and let's talk."

He was grateful for the suggestion. The sight of all the blood had drained his muscles of their strength.

Louisa continued, "Your wife's drain tube simply came loose. I'm surprised it hasn't happened sooner. The GI infection will drain, with or without the tube in place. Your mother-in-law walked in to quite a scare."

Brian remembered Louisa telling them what could happen if the drain came out and how to reinsert new tubing when it did. Because it was all just theory to him, he wasn't sure if he'd even remember how to do it. Plus, it was squeamish work. That open area was difficult to look at, and at times, worse to smell. His MIL did the right thing, calling for Louisa.

"The more important thing is Cassandra's fever. I just took it and it's at 103. I think it's time we got her to the hospital so she can have her port changed. It's infected and it has to come out. I already phoned ahead. An ambulance will be here shortly."

He reached out and gave Louisa's hand a gentle squeeze. "I understand. Thank you." He felt Cassandra's forehead with his other hand and pulled it back as if he'd been shocked. "She was a little warm when I left earlier, but nothing like this."

"She'll get antibiotics in the hospital. The port procedure won't take long. She'll be back home in a few days, once the doctor is confident she's over the infection."

Alice came in with a wet washcloth. She smoothed it over Cassandra's face and neck.

Brian sat back in the chair, exhausted, worried, and waited for the ambulance.

The operation was scheduled for the next day and true to Louisa's word, only took about an hour. They would feed Cassandra IVs of antibiotics and monitor her progress in the hospital. With any luck, she could be back home by the weekend.

Throughout everything, he and Alice spoke very little to one another. They were both tired and nervous, and to be honest, he hadn't been in the mood for small talk. Once the surgeon told them everything was fine, they both exhaled, hugged for a moment, and resumed their comfortable silence.

"I think I'll go stay at my house until Cassie comes home," she'd said when they were leaving the hospital. "I'll make sure the old place is still standing. Besides, I don't want burglars to think no one lives there. Call me the day before they release her so I can be there when she gets home."

"I will," he'd said, feeling the tightness in his stomach.

And now he had the house all to himself.

Which was why he was sitting in the yard for the first time since moving in. He propped himself in his Jets folding camping chair in the center of the yard. He'd found an old, plastic side table in the basement and used it to hold his beer and the newspaper. After cleaning the house, he decided to take a much needed break before heading to the hospital.

He didn't want to be alone in the house, especially when it was silent and he was still.

He didn't want to see the boy; didn't want confirmation that he was crazy or the house was haunted. No matter the answer, he was the loser.

Brian craned his head back and watched an arrow-shaped series of black dots soar across the cloud-filled sky. It seemed impossible that any living creature could fly so incredibly high, so free.

Rolling his neck, he spotted the top half of his reclusive neighbor's snow-white head. She was sitting by the window, maybe watching the geese, too. He waved at the window, not sure if she could even see him, positive she wouldn't respond if he were sitting a foot away.

"Afraid of my house and bordered by Ms. Congeniality," he muttered, taking a sip of beer.

A voice piped up from the opposite yard. "What's that?"

Brian turned to see his other neighbor, he thought his name was Bob or Bill or something close to it. Bob or Bill held electric shears and wore battered work gloves, looking ready for an afternoon of yard work. A stained Giants wool cap was pulled down close to his brow. Brian's own yard cried out for attention, but that was mighty low on his priority list.

"Sorry," Brian said. "Just talking to myself."

"No, I'm the one that's sorry. I saw you waving to Edith in the window and heard you say something and I knew it couldn't be to her. She's not much of a talker."

Brian put his hands on the taut fabric arms of the chair and pushed himself up. He carried his beer to the blue recycling bin and dumped it. He looked at his neighbor over the hedge.

"So it isn't just me," Brian said.

The guy chuckled. "Old Edith hasn't said a word to anyone in as long as I can remember. Even before she got older and infirmed, she kept to herself. The good thing is that you have a neighbor who'll never have wild parties or play the radio too loud. I have been known to get a little crazy on Sundays when the Giants play."

Brian eyed his cap and nodded. "I'm the same way, different team," he replied, gesturing toward his Jets chair.

"Hey, if you want, I could trim a few inches off your bush back there. I'm out here anyway and happy to do it."

"No, you don't have to. You have enough to do." Bill/Bob's yard was twice the size of his own and filled with bushes, small trees and tons of other vegetation that Brian couldn't begin to name.

"Not a problem at all. My wife saw the ambulance the other day. Is your wife okay?"

Brian instinctively pulled inward. It was hard for him to talk about Cassandra's health. He was asked so many times by so many people, he thought it would get easier, like reading from a script. But it was the opposite and sometimes he had to force his emotions back under the surface, cracking a whip like a lion tamer.

"She had to get a little surgery. She'll be back home in a few days." *Please don't ask for more.*

Bob/Bill gave a sympathetic nod and said, "If you ever need anything, just ring our bell and let us know. I said the same thing to your mother-in-law last week. You're part of the neighborhood now. We're a pretty close group. We even have a block party every summer."

"Thanks."

His neighbor smiled and started up the motor on his pruning shears. Brian walked into his house with legs that felt like lead.

I'm afraid to be in my own house, he thought, disappointed with himself.

Then his mind conjured up an image of old Edith, trapped in her own house—shit, trapped in her *own body*. Was it by choice, or was her freedom ripped away from her?

He grabbed his keys off the kitchen counter and headed for the front door.

Thunk!

He stopped at the sound of something falling in the room above.

Brian didn't wait to see if it happened again.

The relentless tug of nerve-shattering agony pulled Cassandra from her deep, dreamless sleep. She always awoke in a state of total confusion, never quite understanding where she was or how she came to be in a strange bed and an even stranger house.

Sometimes, she would recognize her mother or her fiancé, Brian. They would hover over her with painted-on smiles and soft words, but she could never make out what they were saying.

Why is my stomach on fire?

This was always her first thought when coming to.

Why can't I move? Somebody please help. Please make the pain go away.

It was as if her body had mutinied against her, trapping her mind in a shell that refused to obey her commands. The pain and confusion were always there, always intertwined, frightening her until she wanted to escape, back to the black, silent place.

She could see the sunlight on the ceiling, sense that she was alone in this foreign room. But she'd seen this room before. When? Images slipped away faster than they could form.

It feels like someone is stabbing me with a hot poker. Am I dying?

A small shadow draped across her vision.

A pair of cold, emotionless eyes loomed over her. She wanted to scream. Her throat convulsed, opening and closing, but no sounds came out.

Go back, Cass! Back to the empty place!

But the pain wouldn't let her go. It never did. Not until someone came to her and did something magical to make it go away. No one was here to stop her pain now.

No one was here to make those eyes disappear.

CHAPTER FIFTEEN

Cassandra was brought home the following Monday. Principal Mann gave Brian an under-the-table half day to make sure she got settled in right. At least it was good to know he was out of the dog house.

Alice had arrived the night before and was quick to comment about the bags and dark circles under his eyes. He didn't see the need to tell her that he couldn't sleep because he was a grown man afraid of coming face to face again with a little boy.

Louisa thanked the ambulette attendants and triple checked everything. Her every movement around Cassandra was feather light and graceful, like a ballet. He and Alice stood at the foot of the bed while Louisa made sure the drain bag didn't need to be changed.

Cassandra's fever was gone and the waxy complexion had left her face.

"Much better," Louisa said, looking at the new port. "Hopefully she's up and running before this one needs to be replaced."

"She will be," Alice said.

Louisa grinned and said, "That's the right attitude. Cassandra can feel it coming from you as easily as she can hear it."

Brian felt too weary to fake optimism, so he concentrated on

Cassandra, on her pale lips and long eyelashes, the rise and fall of the sheet across her chest, the soft curve of her neck, the skin beating gently with the whooshing of her pulse.

Come back to me. Please.

What Alice said next made his blood freeze. "Just before she went into the hospital, I saw her guardian angel. He was standing right here, watching over her. I know he made the machine go off to get my attention so I would call you. The doctor even said with port infections, every minute is critical." She stared down at her daughter, beaming.

Brian's mouth turned to sand. He managed to sputter, "What...exactly did you see?"

Louisa had stopped putting her things away and couldn't break her gaze from Alice. Brian saw the look of mild concern on the nurse's face.

Alice sighed. "He was an absolute angel. Such a beautiful boy. I even told Father McKenzie about him and he agreed that God has sent someone to watch over Cassie. I can't tell you how much better I've felt about everything."

She looked at Brian and Louisa but seemed to take no note of their stunned expressions. Instead, she said, "I'll make coffee so you two can face your days properly."

Alice sauntered into the kitchen, humming.

Brian had to grip the bedrail for support.

It isn't just me!

His fingertips were numb and his heart felt like it was trying to gallop its way out of his chest. Louisa came to him.

"Brian, are you all right?"

He didn't know what to say. He could only nod.

"Your mother-in-law needed hope, and her mind gave it to her. That's a good thing. She already seems like a different woman. It's nothing to worry about."

Brian was about to tell her it *was* something to worry about when her phone went off. She excused herself and took the call in the living room.

She came back a minute later and slipped her bag over her shoulder. "I have an emergency with a patient in Yonkers. I'll be back tomorrow night. Call me if you need anything."

It took a herculean effort to smile and give a small wave. Alice continued to hum away in the kitchen and chirped a cheerful goodbye.

The boy was real! He wasn't crazy after all.

But what the fuck was he? Was he a guardian angel, like Alice and her agree-to-anything-to-comfort-a-paying-parishioner priest said? If he was, why was Brian so afraid? Shouldn't a guardian angel exude some sense of comfort?

All the boy did was confuse and scare the living hell out of him.

I can't tell Alice that I've seen him. If I do, she'll want to talk about it, and I can't hide the fact that I disagree with her. Listen to her. For the first time in weeks, she's happy, upbeat. You can't lay waste to her hope.

So the secret was out, but it was still very much a secret for him and him alone.

A chill raced up his back.

Is he here now, watching me, watching Alice?

He looked around the room, at Cassandra lying peacefully, wondering if they were ever truly alone.

CHAPTER SIXTEEN

The whispering started three days later.

Brian was shaving. The little radio he'd put on the shelf by the medicine cabinet was tuned to sports talk radio.

His blade was mid-stroke, rising up through the foam from the base of his neck to his jawline when he heard a full but unintelligible sentence in a hushed voice. It came from his right, behind the closed shower curtain. The razor nicked his skin when he pivoted to see where the voice had come from.

"Ah, shit!" He dropped the razor into the full sink.

Holding his finger to the cut on his neck, he grabbed the edge of the vinyl curtain and yanked it to the side.

Empty.

He found the volume knob on the radio and twisted until the sound was off.

He waited for the urgent murmuring to resume. Feeling too naked, exposed, he grabbed a towel and wrapped it around his waist.

The bathroom was silent, save for his labored breath.

Maybe it was something on the radio, he thought. *You just picked up someone talking in the background and thought it was next to you.*

First the phantom boy, who didn't look like any ghost he'd ever heard of, and now this.

After five tense, noiseless minutes, he shook his head and fished around for his razor. He had only ten minutes to get his ass in the car, and zero time to freak himself out.

"Fucking house," he said, wiping the remnants of shaving cream from his face.

Alice was proud of herself. When she'd asked Louisa the other day to go through every little detail on working the infusion pump and the drain, the information really stuck. She even did it all by herself, under Louisa's supervision, without a hitch.

"You *can* teach an old dog new tricks," she'd said to an approving Louisa.

Which was why she didn't feel the urgent need to call Brian and the nurse when she heard Cassie's alarms cry out. Alice was dusting the living room, thinking what to get at the supermarket later, when the first metallic wail went off.

She saw right away that the infusion rate on the pump was off kilter. It had been increased for some reason.

"Damn computers," she said as she pressed the alarm button off and readjusted the setting.

She was startled when she heard the sheets rustling behind her. Cassandra tossed in her sleep, opened her eyes for a moment, then closed them slowly. Her lips parted, and a tiny whimper came out.

"I'm here, honey. I'm here," Alice said, taking her hand.

She stayed with Cassandra for the next hour, casting curious glances at the pump's readout.

Guess I'll have to wait until Brian gets home to get a few things from the store. Don't want that pump changing its settings while I'm out.

At one point Cassandra drew in a sharp breath, and her hand lifted off the bed and wavered to her mouth. Her head turned to the side and her forehead creased with concern.

Alice smoothed her daughter's hair and waited for Brian to return.

The Devils season opener gave Brian something light to focus on and forget things for a couple of hours. The TV was still in his bedroom, and he settled in the chair next to Cassandra to watch the game.

Despite the changing of the port and the clearing of her infection, she didn't seem to be getting any better. She'd been awake a few hours earlier and he'd tried to talk to her, but her eyes were like frozen, muddy puddles and there was no recognition of her husband.

When she was in the hospital, even Dr. Stepka had said he was surprised she wasn't more awake, more lucid.

The sole positive Brian could see at this point was that the mysterious boy hadn't made an appearance since Cassandra's return from the hospital. It bothered him that he couldn't stop from fixating on their child visitor, not when Cassandra's life was in the balance. Maybe it was the *ghost's*, for lack of a better word, own fixation with his wife that kept the wheels churning in his brain.

"Pad save and a beaut!" the Devils' play-by-play man exclaimed. It shook Brian from his troubled thoughts.

"You should have seen that one, Cass. What a save," he said.

They were both Devils fans, a pair of nonconformists living in Ranger territory. He tried every season to get to at least five or more games. Cassandra loved hockey, and even more so in person at the arena.

The score popped up on the screen. Devils 2—Flyers 1. Brian hit the mute button before the commercial started. If he couldn't skip through them, he damn well didn't need to hear them.

He picked up the empty popcorn bowl on the floor by his feet and got up to put it in the sink. Alice was upstairs reading, so the bottom floor was bathed in darkness. He padded across the floor and banged his knee on the edge of the kitchen table.

The voice came from directly behind him.

Brian whirled around and almost smacked his nose into the refrigerator.

Again, he couldn't tell what had been said. It sounded like the voice of a woman, whispering a few short words.

Or a child.

Creeping dread prickled the base of Brian's skull.

Was the boy here? All he had to do was peer around the edge of the kitchen doorway to see.

The thought of walking back to his bedroom made him lightheaded.

The floor creaked above and his shoulders hitched.

Has to be Alice moving in bed.

He took a hesitant step, pausing to listen for more barely audible mumbling. The hush of the house was overwhelming. It was like surfing; that moment when you lost your balance and tipped into the cold, wild spray. Until you broke the surface, you were smothered by the merciless ocean, helpless in its grip.

Brian sucked in a ragged breath.

I'll just poke my head into the hallway and see if he's there. If he is, I'll deal with it.

His body wasn't as gung-ho with the idea as his mind. It was an effort to take another step, to place a steadying hand on the kitchen counter, to move his back and neck those precious inches so he could see into the hallway.

A dark yet empty hall stretched out before him. The flickering blue light of the TV bled across its walls. There was no boy, no expectant specter or guardian angel.

"Jesus Christ," Brian said, exhaling the breath he hadn't realized he'd been holding. "This is getting ridiculous."

A low, stressed moan came from the bedroom. It was Cassandra.

Brian forgot his fear and walked down the hallway to check on his wife.

Halfway there, something came close to his ear and whispered, *"Briiiiaaaaannnnn."*

His joints locked and the hairs on the back of his neck went rigid.

It was a boy's voice, high, soft, almost playful.

He was either right by his side or behind him. This time, Brian couldn't make himself look.

The sudden blaring of the TV made him jump back, breaking his paralysis. He ran the rest of the way and into the bedroom where he hit the mute button again. The remote control was where he'd left it, on his chair and out of Cassandra's reach.

Brian's insides burned hot with terror, but his skin was cold and clammy. Fumbling with the remote, he turned and again saw nothing but an empty hallway. His breath came in short, pained gasps.

"Uhhhhh."

Cassandra's eyes were open, glazed and bloodshot, the once vibrant color faded, washed away by the sickness eating away at her and the drugs used to keep her comfortable and alive. Brian crouched over her and cupped the side of her face in his hand.

Her lips twitched into something resembling a smile.

"Hey you," he said, his voice shaking. "Did you wake up to watch the Devils game with me?" He smiled and knew how terribly false it must look.

Cassandra turned her head, each inch seeming to take an eternity. Brian stroked her cheek, wiping a small tear that had leaked from the corner of her eye. When her gaze fell upon the open doorway, she sucked in a great lungful of air, closed her eyes, and fell back into limbo.

Still keeping his hand on her to let her know he was with her, Brian reached out with his foot and pulled the door closed, shutting out the hallway.

CHAPTER SEVENTEEN

When Tony got the call from Mrs. Torre to take Brian out, he was only too happy to oblige. She answered the door and pulled him by the arm, closing the door quickly behind him.

"Brian's in the back room with Cassie. Here's fifty dollars." She pressed the bills into his hand. "Take him to a bar and have some drinks. He needs to blow off some steam."

Tony handed the money back to her. "You don't have to pay me to take him to a bar. I'm just glad he's finally ready to go out for a little bit, you know. He's gotta take care of himself, too."

Alice Torre bit her lower lip and scrunched her eyes. "The thing is, he doesn't know I called you over. I want you to go in there and convince him to get out of the house for a bit."

"Oh boy. This sounds like a forced blind date."

She placed her hands on his back and guided him to the back bedroom. "Go."

Tony knocked on the door.

Brian said, "You can come in, MIL. We're just watching TV."

He opened the door and was stunned by the appearance of his two closest friends. Cassandra was in bed, eyes closed as usual, but her skin color was off, a shade between gray and yellow. The flesh of her face had been pulled tight until she looked like a tribal death mask. It scared the hell out of him, seeing her that way.

Brian was no better. He'd lost weight. His eyes were ringed by dark circles and it even looked like his hair was thinning. If Tony didn't know better, he'd swear Brian was the one who'd been in and out of the hospital.

"Holy shit, what are you doing here?" Brian said.

Tony couldn't tell whether his friend was happily shocked or perturbed. Maybe both. He pulled him in for a hug, felt the new frailty in Brian's frame.

"I've come to whisk you away for the night, bro. Mrs. T. has the graveyard shift. I've met a lot of people who need a drink, and none of them needed one as bad as you do. Come on, we'll head over to Doug's and have a few."

For a moment, a frightening pall washed over Brian's face. He looked like an animal trapped in a corner. Then it was gone, replaced by a skeletal smile that would scare the pants off of little trick-or-treaters.

"I don't know if I should," he said.

Tony clapped him on the shoulder. "You should and you will. Now go make yourself presentable. Can't believe I have to say that when I'm taking you to Doug's dive."

Brian's shoulders sagged, and he nodded. "You're right. I'll just be a minute." He left to head to the bathroom.

Tony looked down at Cassandra, and his heart broke. "What's happening to the both of you?" he whispered.

Something flickered out of the corner of his eye. He turned to face an empty room.

He bent forward and kissed Cassandra's forehead. "I promise not to have him out late tonight. You get better. We all miss you."

Brian woke up in the middle of the night with an aching bladder. It was nice, Tony taking him to Doug's, but the beer was crying to be let out. Getting off the air mattress and erect was no easy task. The room spun in a half circle and his temples felt like firecrackers had exploded beneath the surface.

He stumbled around Cassandra's bed and made it to the bathroom, each step an angry punch to his dehydrated skull. Not trusting his aim, he sat on the toilet, dropping his head into his hands.

They had run into a bunch of people he knew at the bar, including Andi, Cassandra's friend from the office who'd been in their wedding party. For brief moments, he forgot about Cassandra and the boy, but no amount of beer could take him completely away from his troubled thoughts.

Shambling back into his room, he collapsed on the mattress. It made a ton of noise, but Cassandra didn't move.

Settling back to sleep, his ears still rang from the loud music at the bar and everyone shouting to be heard above it. A little white noise always worked to take his mind off it so he could sleep. Tonight, it was too quiet to drown out the whining in his ears.

Wait, why is it so quiet?

He shot up on the mattress and it felt like his head took an extra second to catch up with the rest of his body.

Looking over the bed, he saw that the infusion pump was dark.

"Dammit," he muttered.

No matter what buttons he pressed, it was dead.

"What the hell?"

Did we have a power outage?

He flicked the overhead light and the brightness seared his eyes. Okay, so power wasn't the problem. Maybe the machine just died. Brian turned on the small Hello Kitty lamp, went to wash his hands, and came back to disconnect the hyperal. Cassandra would be all right until morning without it.

When he opened the medical waste bin, he saw a good length of the power cord snaking out from under the bed. Dropping to his hands and knees, he followed the path of the cord until he came to the outlet.

It was unplugged.

Did he trip across it during his drunken walk to the bathroom? But that would have been impossible. The cord was kept out of the way so just that kind of thing couldn't happen. And what about the backup battery?

He got up and checked the battery compartment. The battery was connected, but there was no way to tell if it had any juice left in it.

The headache that had been building had reached an intolerable crescendo. It hurt too much to concentrate on getting the hyperal hooked back up. He set the alarm for 6:00 a.m. and tried to get a few hours' sleep. His brain wouldn't shut down.

How did it get unplugged? It would have tripped me if my foot got caught.

He'd taken to closing the door day and night, not wanting to even glance into the hallway by accident.

No. Not possible.

He shuddered under the blanket, staring up at Cassandra's bed until dawn.

CHAPTER EIGHTEEN

Louisa had asked Brian if she could take his blood pressure, but he'd refused. Instead, he'd said he had to get something out of his car. He didn't look well. She'd often seen caregivers fall into worse situations than the patients because they didn't take proper care of themselves. Stress took years off their lives.

She replaced the battery on the infusion pump and took Cassandra's pulse. Weak but steady.

"All fixed?" Alice asked.

Louisa was equally worried about Cassandra's mother. If Brian was in free fall, Alice was buoyed to the point that Louisa was concerned she could no longer see the present situation with any sort of clarity. The higher she went, the worse the fall should Cassandra take a bad turn.

And last was Cassandra. By all rights, she should be better by now. Less and less of the infection was draining from her and the worst was in the rearview mirror. But still she slumbered on like Sleeping Beauty, with one twist; her prince was by her side and even his kiss couldn't bring her back.

"Yes," Louisa replied. "I tested it several times and the battery is fully charged and switches on if I disconnect the AC power. There shouldn't be any problems."

Brian entered the room looking harried. He said, "I had some signed forms for you, Louisa, and I thought I left them in the car, but I guess I didn't. Maybe they're on my dresser." He riffled through a stack of paper-clipped documents.

She sidled next to him and asked, "You want some help? I can spot my company's paperwork from a mile off."

Alice said, "You know, Brian, I thought I saw you put them in that box in the closet. Aren't they the ones you were working on the other night?"

"Yeah, those were the ones," he said.

Alice walked to the closet and pulled out a plastic tub. It was filled to the top with medical and insurance forms.

Louisa heard the floor pop twice behind her and turned to see if something had fallen out of her bag. She saw a young boy turn his back on them and walk silently out of the room. She took three quick steps to see where he went, but he'd disappeared.

When Brian yelped, "Found 'em!" she gasped.

"Sorry, didn't mean to scare you," he said.

Louisa finally understood. She needed to talk to Brian, alone.

"No, I'm fine. My mind just wandered off for a bit. Why don't you walk me to my car and I'll make sure I get everything to the office?"

"Sounds good. Let me get my coat. I have to head out to the store anyway."

The air was unseasonably cold and damp. It felt like the dead of winter, not mid-fall. Louisa pulled the zipper on her leather coat as high as it could go, took Brian's medical forms and dropped them in an accordion folder she kept in her back seat.

She wasn't sure how she was going to break the news to him or how he would take it, but she couldn't leave and not say anything. He needed to understand what was in his house and why.

The direct approach would have to do.

"Brian, I hope you don't mind if I tell you something very important."

She saw the color drain from his face and had to address the alarm in his expression.

"It's nothing bad about Cassandra," she said, and his chest deflated.

"You scared me for a second there." Vapor tailed from his mouth in winding wisps.

Louisa gathered her resolve, took a breath and said, "I just saw the boy."

His eyelids lowered. She could see his jaw tense. His lips pulled tight, and he leaned against her car.

He's seen it too!

When he didn't say anything, she continued, "I watched a boy leave the room while you and Alice were looking for the paperwork. Brian, that isn't a guardian angel."

He looked down at the cracked sidewalk and said, "I know. I've seen him a few times. There's nothing angelic about him...or *it*. I haven't told Alice because I don't want to bring her down." His eyes locked with hers, and she could see the fear and sadness behind them. "Do you know what it is?"

She nodded. An older woman pushing a metal cart walked between them, on her way to the markets along Katonah Avenue.

"In my country, we call what's in your house a *bhoot*. They're trapped souls. For one reason or another, they can't move on to the next phase of death. I'm telling you this because I don't want you to be afraid of him. That boy...you only see him because he suffers. He can't harm you or Cassandra. Maybe one day, when you're both well, you can help relieve him of his pain."

Brian snorted. "That sounds crazier than seeing a ghost boy walking around the house. How the heck can I help the suffering of a trapped soul?"

Louisa placed a reassuring hand on his arm. "I understand how you feel. To you, this is the stuff of bad movies and TV shows. In my culture, bhoots are common. There is so much suffering in India, and some souls can't shed the pain they endured in life. This boy is either attached to the house or one of you. Maybe he sees something in you or Alice or Cassandra that feels comforting."

Brian's stare was far away. "He keeps going to Cassandra. Ever since I started seeing him, things have been happening to her life support machine. You say a bhoot can't harm us. I'm not so sure."

"A bhoot is incorporeal, Brian. That boy is not part of the physical world. It's frightening to look at, but when you realize what you are seeing and what he really is, there's no need to fear him."

She didn't feel comfortable not telling him the entire truth, but he was in no state to hear about the varied aspects of the bhoot. It was true that the vast majority of bhoots were as harmless as they were formless. There were also stories of bhoots, shades of evil people, who were malicious, eager to strike out at the living. Sometimes it was directed at a person who they felt had wronged them in life; other times, they took nefarious pleasure in terrifying anyone in their sight.

The chimera of the boy could not be this way. Children, even the naughty ones, were innocent by nature.

An icy gust of wind swept through the narrow street like the rushing tide of a tsunami. The chill cut through her heavy coat.

Brian's mouth opened slightly, then closed again. She could see there was more he wanted to say. Maybe more he had to reveal? This was a delicate subject and she knew not to prod him. He would tell her what he wanted her to know, in his time.

She said, "You have my number. Please call me any time. It doesn't only have to be when you need help with your wife. I don't want you to be afraid."

"I'm not convinced, but I am glad you saw him, too. It makes me feel less crazy."

He sputtered a sad, short-lived laugh.

"I'll be back the day after tomorrow," Louisa said. "The next time you see the boy, try talking to him, let him know you're not afraid. Ask him what he wants. He just may answer you and give you the key to putting him to rest."

Brian looked skeptical. He said, "You better get in the car. It's freezing out here. See you in a couple of days."

She drove away, watching him watching her in the rearview mirror until she turned at the end of the street and he faded out of sight.

CHAPTER NINETEEN

Alice surprised him that night by making his favorite, pasta fagioli. The smell of simmering onions and spices perfumed every corner of the house.

Ever since his talk with Louisa, he'd been wrapped in his own thoughts, trying to puzzle out why this ghost boy, or bhoot, was in his home and fixated on Cassandra. Alice mistook his consternation for depression and announced she was going to do something that would cheer him up.

The beans were tender and the pasta al dente.

He slurped down a spoonful and said, "MIL, you've outdone yourself. I could eat five bowls."

"It's great to see your appetite is back. If you want six bowls, I'll fill it each time for you. Just eat." She smiled, barely touching her own bowl. Like all good Italian mothers, she was always on the alert, waiting to see if there was anything else she could get to make him happy. He suspected this was how most Italian moms stayed so thin.

"I'm sorry I've been so distant, especially today," Brian said. "I've just got a lot on my mind."

"No apologies. You have more on your plate than any boy your age should have. I'm just glad I can help a little bit."

A large, fast-moving shadow raced past the kitchen doorway and down the hall.

They both saw it. Alice's spoon clattered into her bowl.

Brian pushed back from the table, the chair scraping against the tile floor.

"What was that?" Alice asked.

"I don't know." He walked to the hall and wasn't surprised this time to find it empty. He'd left the door to the bedroom open and saw that Cassandra's bedside was devoid of visitors.

"Maybe someone walked past the kitchen window and the shadow came in here," Alice said behind him. He noticed how reticent she was to join him in the hall.

He looked at the kitchen window and shook his head. The white shade was pulled all the way down and patterned curtains blocked out anything that could seep in through the sides.

Alice looked frightened, so he said, "That's probably it. You see that big Doberman the people in the three-family house own? Maybe he got off his leash and is running around."

That seemed to put her at ease, though there was still a glimmer of doubt in her eyes. "That thing needs a saddle, not a leash," she said.

They finished dinner in silence.

Alice took a quick run to the small grocery store on Katonah

Avenue. Since moving in with Brian and Cassandra, she'd become addicted to the sweet Irish butter and scones. It seemed she was the one woman in the store without an Irish brogue. She felt alien. But all that really mattered was that she had something to snack on for the afternoon.

Back in the house, she slathered a scone with butter, poured a cup of coffee, and decided she'd read to Cassandra. She'd been reading a Harlan Coben book to her the past week and was already on chapter sixteen. Alice liked to think they were both hooked on the story.

"Now where did I put my glasses?" She'd last been reading the paper in the living room earlier, but they weren't on the table.

Things had been moving to places they didn't belong almost from the moment she'd walked into this house. At first, she'd assumed it was just her and Brian being forgetful because they had more pressing things occupying their thoughts.

After seeing the boy and talking to Father McKenzie, she was convinced that Cassandra's diminutive guardian angel was misplacing items to get their attention. In fact, since acknowledging him, everything had been in its proper place.

She checked her room, then the bathroom to cover her bases. Walking to the landing so she could look in Cassandra and Brian's room, the sound of heavy, quick footsteps coming *up* the stairs made her jump back. Her hands flew to her mouth, and she stifled a scream.

Someone's in the house!

They're coming and I can't even make myself move!

Any second, a strange man—a thief, a murderer—was going to pop up the stairs, see her in her helpless state of rigidity, and make her pay for being a witness to his crime.

The footsteps continued, but no one emerged from the stairway.

Suddenly, it stopped. The top step creaked under the weight of an invisible presence, then went silent.

Alice held her breath. Her heart went into arrhythmia and she had to exhale to settle it down.

No one was there.

"Hello?" Her voice shook. The muscles in her legs turned to jelly.

"Hello." This time louder. Her periphery grew dark and fuzzy.

"Hello!"

Only the sound of Cassandra's life support machine answered.

CHAPTER TWENTY

When Alice told him about the phantom footsteps, he asked, "Do you think it was Cass's guardian angel?" It took a lot to not sound condescending.

"I've been praying on it all day. If it was, why would it want to scare me like that?"

Brian sat in the love seat opposite her. It had been a long day and all he wanted to do was eat and turn in early. The lack of sleep and food was catching up with him. He stayed late to work with the kids who would be on the baseball team in the spring. Showing them warm-up exercises had left him winded, and worried.

Seeing Alice in such a state made him realize it was time to come clean.

He chose his next words with care. "Have you considered that the boy you saw wasn't a guardian angel?"

She shook her head, then leaned back on the sofa and closed her eyes. "Not until today, no."

"Would it make you feel better if I told you I've been seeing him, too?"

Her eyes snapped open. "Why didn't you tell me?"

"I have plenty of reasons, one of them being that I didn't want you or anyone else to think I'd lost it. I have to be strong for Cassandra." He got up and paced around the area rug. "I didn't say a word when you proclaimed it to be Cass's guardian angel because I saw how much faith it gave you that she would be all right. Even though what *I* felt when I saw him wasn't close to comforting."

"How many times have you seen him?"

"More than I wanted to. And that's not including the noises, the shadows, the whispering."

"Whispering?" Alice clutched a throw pillow against her chest.

"That started recently, since Cass's port was changed. One night, I swear I thought I heard my name. It scared the shit out of me. But what can I do? This is my house. I won't let some ghost boy chase me out. Louisa even told me to talk to it. She called it a bhoot. She said it was some kind of trapped, tortured soul. Maybe if I talk to it, I can find out why it's here and help set it free. Can you imagine me talking to a fucking ghost?"

"How…how does Louisa know?"

It felt like a dam had burst inside him and there was no stopping the flow. He was going to let everything out until he was empty.

"She saw it, too. Of course, she's not afraid of it because she's not living with it. In India, she says these things are common. Well, this sure as hell isn't India. So now I have a bhoot that's obsessed with my wife. My poor goddamn wife who gets worse and worse every day and who I would kill to talk to for just five minutes. And here I am with a job with no sick or vacation days left, bills up my ass, and a future in bankruptcy court. When I thought the boy was a product of my imagination, I was fine with it. Insanity I can understand. It can be fixed. But this, whatever the fuck it is. I…I…"

The words piled up in a tangled jumble and he couldn't force them out. Instead, he grabbed a vase full of carnations and smashed it against the front door.

Alice looked at him not with horror or anger but consolation. She moved the pillow aside and got up from the couch. He was breathing heavy and cords of tension twisted at the base of his neck. Without saying a word, she pulled him to her. At first, he was so riled and knotted with anger that he was afraid to put his arms around her; worried he might crush her.

Her warmth and comfort helped bleed off his frustration. He settled down and returned her embrace.

"We'll face it together," she said, her face pressed against his chest. "It'll be two versus one from now on, you hear me?"

Brian could smell the fading scent of shampoo in her hair. "Yeah."

They squeezed each other when the house shook with the sound of a slamming door.

"What was that?" Alice said, breaking away from him.

He looked down the hallway, saw that the door to his bedroom was shut.

"That was my door. I think someone didn't like what we just said."

He ran down the hall and pulled the door open. Alice was close behind.

Cassandra was the only one in the room. The slamming of the door hadn't disturbed her at all.

Brian looked around the room, felt the anger rising in him again. For weeks, he'd thought if he could just punch someone, break something, it would release the pressure. It was finally coming out, and it felt good.

"You want to play games?" he said, turning in a tight circle to address the four corners of the room. "I don't know who or what you are, but I want you to leave us the hell alone. I didn't invite you here. I don't care about your suffering. My wife is suffering. We're suffering. The whole goddamn world suffers!"

His voice rose until he was shouting. He felt Alice tug on his arm.

"Why don't you get the fuck out of here, huh? I don't believe you're some lost little boy. I think that's what you want us to see. Leave...my wife...alone! You're not welcome. Go find someplace else to haunt."

When he felt like there was nothing left to say, no epithets to hurl, he stopped to catch his breath.

He and Alice looked down the hall, listening for any odd sounds above the hum of Cassandra's life support machine.

The house remained silent.

But Brian would swear on his grandmother's grave that it was far from empty.

CHAPTER TWENTY-ONE

As Brian dragged the heavy plastic garbage pail to the curb, he thought he heard someone call out to him. He looked over at Bill/Bob's house and didn't see anyone.

"Great, you're following me out here, too?" he said, low enough so no one nearby would realize he was talking to himself.

He was stunned to see Edith, his silent elderly neighbor, sitting on the porch, motioning to him.

He pointed at his chest. *Who, me?*

She nodded, the great mane of gray hair blocking much of her face.

Can't wait to tell Bill/Bob about this one, he thought.

Flipping the metal latch on her front gate, he walked to the bottom of her wood steps.

"Is there something I can help you with?" he asked.

She wagged a gnarled, arthritic finger. Up close he could see the deep lines on her face, the weariness in her eyes. Her jowls hung loosely off her skull. She looked far older than her eighty plus years.

"Are you all right, son?" she asked with a voice as thin as a reed.

The question took him by surprise. "Yes, I'm fine. How are *you?*"

"I heard shouting the other night. I don't like shouting. I thought it might have been you. Angry with someone?"

Fantastic. Now the neighbors could hear me screaming at our ghost. She must have heard the vase explode, too. That would be enough to frighten a lonely old woman.

"Just blowing off a little steam. Nothing to worry about. By the way, my name's Brian."

She ignored his outstretched hand and instead said, "Is everything okay with the house?"

It seemed an innocuous, neighborly kind of question, but coming from a woman who never spoke, Brian felt there had to be more to it.

"Yes...it's fine. Still settling in. We have a long way to go."

"Is your wife the sick one?"

It pained him to have her labeled like that. *The sick one.* "Yes. She's home recovering. Hopefully you can meet her soon."

"I see ambulances and people come and go."

He didn't know how to respond to that other than to nod his head.

It was a long while before she spoke again. Brian turned to go, uncomfortable and assuming she was finished with him, but she raised a finger, keeping his feet planted on the steps.

She said, "Why don't you make yourself useful and help me out of this chair? My knees have a tendency to lock."

He reached out to hold her leathery hands and she pulled them back. "What do you want to do, pull my arms out of their sockets? If you're going to help, you have to lift me."

This close, he could smell the sharp tang of her body odor, as well as the overpowering scent of, for lack of a better word, *old*. If sepia had a smell, this would be it. It was the odor of a life coming full circle, of memories and regrets, of a body preparing to go home. Placing his arms around her waist, he locked his hands together behind her back and lifted. She felt light as a puppy in his arms. Edith in turn placed her arms around him and grunted as he got her to her feet. He handed the cane by the chair to her.

"All set?" he asked.

Her heavy lids drooped over her wet, rheumy eyes, and she turned to shuffle into the house.

I'll take that as a 'yes, and thanks for the help, young man,' Brian thought.

When Brian came back inside, Alice was sitting on the couch doing her crossword. Like him, she looked tired, but also like him, she needed to keep her hands and mind busy, lest she let the dark tendrils of fear and doubt overtake her. Brian thought of the way they felt in terms of a line from an old Aerosmith song: *"Tap dancing on a land mine."*

They went through their daily motions: getting ready, going to work, caring for Cass, cleaning the house, shopping, and on and on. Each moment was pregnant with expectation.

Is the boy just around the corner?

Is he behind me?

What was that sound? Was it a whisper? Did something move?

What's that thing that just moved out of the corner of my eye? A trick of light? Are my eyes just tired?

Or worse.

Throughout each day, little things happened in every corner of the house. Brian and Alice had been on high alert, hearts jumping into their throats at the slightest sound.

It's playing with us, Brian said to himself one night when three footsteps tapped outside the closed bedroom door. *It knows it has us right on the edge.*

Alice looked up from her puzzle and said, "I just checked on Cassie and lasagna's in the oven."

Brian hung his coat on the hook by the door. "Thanks. I just spoke to our neighbor." He pointed with his thumb over his right shoulder.

"The old lady?"

"The one and only Edith. She heard me shouting at you-know-what the other night. Apparently, she doesn't like loud noises."

"Well, maybe that broke the ice."

"I doubt it. She asked me a couple of questions, then clammed up. I think she exhausted her word count for the year."

Brian headed upstairs but stopped when he saw Alice's stunned expression. He turned to see what she was looking at.

Beside the front door was a window looking out onto the porch. Cassandra had said she was going to buy a small table to put by the window so she could display fresh flowers every day. The only things under the window now were a pile of unpacked cardboard boxes, filled with books and summer clothes.

The narrow, plastic knob that controlled the blinds moved counterclockwise. The blinds slowly closed, shutting out the dying light of the day.

"That's a new one," Brian said. "Saved me from having to do it myself." He was too tired to be scared. He hoped mocking the ghost's actions would piss it off. Maybe if they showed it they weren't afraid, it would move on.

A steady murmur caught his attention, but it was only Alice. Her hands were clasped together on her lap. A succession of Hail Marys tumbled from her lips.

The house groaned like an old, ocean-battered schooner.

It's pulling everything out of its bag of tricks.

He said, "MIL, why don't you come upstairs with me?"

She stopped her prayers and nearly leapt off the couch.

He caught her frightened eyes and said, "Look, you don't have to stay here if you don't want to. I understand. If you want to take Cassandra to your house, I'm fine with that. Maybe that would be best, so we know she's safe."

Alice clutched the newel post and scanned the room. "No matter where we take Cassie, it'll follow her."

He knew somehow that she was right. He'd been mulling the truth over the past several weeks, but it didn't hit home until Alice said it aloud. It wasn't the house that was haunted. It was Cassandra. All the other theatrics were meant to chase him and Alice away, so the bhoot could have her to itself.

That wasn't going to happen.

CHAPTER TWENTY-TWO

The weather report on 1010WINS was dire. What was at first a Nor'easter heading their way had picked up strength from another storm off the coast of North Carolina and turned into a sizeable hurricane.

Every borough of the city was on alert. It would make landfall sometime after the evening rush hour the next day.

"It's kind of late in the season to have a hurricane," Alice said over toast and coffee.

Brian had been kind enough to move her mattress into his and Cassie's bedroom after the incident with the blinds. It gave her some level of comfort, not being upstairs, alone, but she still got very little sleep.

"I can't remember the last time we had a hurricane warning in the Bronx," Brian said. "Strange weather. I'm going to head over to Home Depot after work to pick up a generator. If it hits, I don't want to be without power for longer than the battery life in the infusion pump."

"I'll call Louisa and make sure she stops by to check on Cassie."

Brian put his dish and coffee mug in the sink. "I don't even know what the hell I'm supposed to do to prepare for a hurricane. I live in the Bronx, so I don't have to worry about this kind of stuff."

"I doubt it'll be that strong but you should get duct tape, batteries and candles to be safe."

"What's the duct tape for?"

"To tape the windows so they don't shatter. I used to summer in the Keys when I was a kid. We were always getting ready for storms."

"Got it. Call me if you need me."

The moment he left, Alice went back to the bedroom. She didn't want to leave her daughter's side. She opened the Harlan Coben book and picked up where she'd left off.

Cassandra heard her mother's voice, but it was so far off. It reminded her of the time she'd taken the pedal boat out too far on the lake when they went to Maine on vacation. She hadn't realized just how far she'd gone until she detected her mother's faint voice carried on the gentle wind. She'd been able to see her, a small speck on the sand, but she couldn't make out the words.

Just like now.

Why can't I open my eyes?

She felt like she should be awake. Was she dreaming? The terrible pain wasn't stabbing her stomach, so maybe she was asleep.

But the pain is only gone when I'm in the dark place.

Mom, can you hear me?

I want to wake up. I can hear you, Mom.

I can hear you.

Something else was holding her prisoner. Something greater and more powerful than the pain.

Let me go. Please, let me go. I want to wake up. I want to hold my mother. Where's Brian?

I remember!

We're married. Oh, I was so sick, all through the ceremony and the reception. We had our first dance. I couldn't touch my dinner. Couldn't think of putting anything in my stomach.

They wheeled the cake over.

"And promise you won't smash it all over my face."

He smiled and there was mischief in those eyes, the eyes she wanted to stare into forever.

And then the agony.

Then nothing.

Fragments of sounds, scraps of memories, and always, the torment.

I want to wake up!

It took a lot of cursing and knuckle scraping to get the generator in place. Brian hoped he didn't have to use it, but he was damned sure to put it together the right way just in case.

It had set him back five-hundred dollars. It was money he didn't have to spare, so he put it on the last credit card that had money left on it.

When he was done, he checked on Cassandra. Her face was covered in sweat and her skin looked so pale. She didn't have a fever. It almost looked like the kind of sweat you'd work up on a long run. But Cass wasn't running anywhere.

He used a damp washcloth to wash her face and changed her sheets to get her more comfortable.

Alice was working like a line chef in the kitchen.

"If we lose power, I don't want this food to go to waste. We'll eat up tonight and tomorrow."

"I'll do what I can." He didn't have the heart to tell her he wasn't the least bit hungry.

The weather outside was calm. There wasn't a cloud in the sky and the temperature had gone up ten degrees from the day before. All signs that the worst was coming.

Tomorrow was a Saturday. At least he'd be home when it hit. His school was built to be a bomb shelter, so he doubted they'd close it if it came today. The kids were safer in the gym than their houses.

"Oh, I picked up the nutmeg you asked for," he said.

He grabbed his coat off the wall peg and rooted around his pocket for the bottle.

His fingers closed around a square of paper. When he pulled his hand out, he saw it was actually two pieces of yellowed newspaper, folded over many times.

Carefully unfolding the papers, he watched the smaller one fall to the floor. A *NY Daily News* headline, dated November 12, 1958, read:

MERCY KILLING LEAVES POLICE DUMBFOUNDED

In a bizarre act of love, a nine-year-old Bronx boy turned off his mother's iron lung. She died shortly thereafter. Mrs. Margaret Thomas had been suffering from polio for the past several years. In the final stages of the disease, she was placed in an iron lung earlier this year. Her son, James Thomas, was overheard by reporters saying, "I didn't want her to hurt anymore. Can I see her now?" Family members were too distraught for comment, and police have taken young James into custody. A judge will have to decide his fate in what can only be described as an act of mercy gone terribly wrong.

Brian's hands trembled as he read the rest of the article. Most of it was speculation on what would happen to the boy. He laid it on the arm of the couch and stooped to pick up the smaller article. It was dated January 5, 1959.

MORE TRAGEDY FOR BRONX FAMILY

Nine-year old James Thomas, who came to our attention last November when he disabled his mother's life support machine, accidentally killing her, has also died at a tragically young age of complications from pneumonia. He had been allowed back in his home after his headline making arrest and subsequent release. The courts deemed him too young to be charged as an adult. The young boy, who only wanted to ease his mother's suffering, didn't realize the fatal consequences of his actions. "I hope he's at peace now, with his mother," said his father, Daniel Thomas, in a brief and teary statement. James was his only child.

Brian felt the world slip out from under him. He collapsed onto the couch, holding an article in each hand.

Where the hell did these come from?

He looked at Alice in the kitchen, browning sausages in a pan. No, it couldn't have been her.

Who else had access to his coat? Was it a teacher in school? But why?

He was finding it hard to take a breath. He looked back down at the article on James Thomas's death.

Oh my God.

> *The tragedy occurred at 124 Buckingham Road. Friends and neighbors are in a state of shock at the news of young James's premature death.*

124 Buckingham Road.

It happened in this house.

> *James is survived by his father, Daniel Thomas, and his uncle and aunt, Paul and Edith Thomas, who reside in the neighboring home.*

Edith Thomas! She must have slipped them in his pocket when he picked her up out of her chair.

"We brought him back," Brian said.

"What's that honey?" Alice called out from the kitchen.

"We brought him back, and he thinks Cassandra is his mother."

He rose from the couch, walking on legs that didn't feel attached to his body, opened the door and sprinted to Edith's front door. He rang the bell, knocked loudly, but there was no answer. Every window in the house was dark.

A loud current of wind whistled down the street, blowing the lid off a metal garbage can in someone's yard.

Edith had said all she was going to say.

It was his job now to stop the boy from repeating the same mistake.

CHAPTER TWENTY-THREE

Louisa came in the morning when most people were shuttering themselves up for the day. She gave Cassandra and her life support a thorough examination. Brian sat in the room with her the entire time, wrapped in his own thoughts.

She noticed the second mattress in the room and was concerned, but knew not to probe.

When she was finished, Brian said, "Louisa, can I show you something?"

"Of course."

"You might want to take a seat."

He handed a pair of old news articles to her. She placed her bag on the floor and opened them up.

Oh dear.

When she was done, she felt terrible for not telling him everything about the bhoot. Worse still, she felt sick to her stomach knowing they had something far worse to face than a simple lost soul.

"Brian, you can't leave Cassandra's side, especially not tonight. The storm is full of energy. A bhoot thrives on the power of nature. The boy will be strong tonight. His obsession with Cassandra can be harmful. Because of what James Thomas did to his mother, he can never be reunited with her. He sees your wife as his mother, all over again. He's just a boy. He'll repeat what he did if given the chance. As long as Cassandra remains close to death, she's vulnerable."

Brian rubbed his hands across his face. "What do I do? How do I convince him that she's not his goddamn mother?"

Louisa felt pressure around her heart. She reached out to him and said, "You can't. He won't listen to you. He wants Cassandra. Right now, she's in a place that's not quite life, not quite death. It's a place where the bhoot can grab hold of her. She's in his domain. She's the one person who can fight him off, if she has the spiritual strength."

Her words seemed to sap away what little stamina he had left. His mouth hung open and he stared at Cassandra with lost, helpless eyes.

"Be with her," she said. "When the boy appears, keep talking to her. Let her know you're here, waiting for her. Tell her not to be tricked by the boy. Do whatever you can to keep her from slipping away." She felt hot tears well in the corners of her eyes.

Brian looked angry, but not at her.

"None of this seems real," he said. "A part of me keeps saying it *can't* be real. I know that's just wishful thinking."

"Don't let her go, Brian. When the time comes, bring her back to you."

She left him sitting on the bed with his wife, his fingers entwined with hers.

When Louisa was back in her car, her body shook with chills and her teeth chattered so hard they hurt. She'd told Brian she would be back tomorrow. She prayed they would get through the night.

The rain came first. The skies went from sunny to pitch black in minutes. Rain lashed against the house in driving buckets.

"Alice, we have to talk."

Brian called her into the bedroom. He sat at the foot of Cassandra's hospital bed. Alice looked worried.

"There's something I need to tell you."

He tried not to sound as bone weary as he felt. If he had to be strong tonight, he would be. And so would his MIL.

He told her about Edith slipping the articles in his coat and gave them to her. There were tears in her eyes as she read them. He told her what Louisa had said, and how the boy would try to take her from them to ease her suffering, just as he did to his mother.

"She said that because he had killed his mother, even though it was an accident, he could never be with her in the afterlife. He thinks Cassandra is his second chance. We can't let that happen."

"What do we do?"

"We keep Cassandra grounded, here. It's all we can do."

The house's frame popped as a gust of wind slammed into it. They heard the *thunk* of lawn chairs that had been left unsecured, scattering between narrow alleys.

Brian said, "We'll eat in here and make sure she's never alone. We need to keep our strength up and keep talking to her. That sound like a plan?"

Alice nodded. "I have to go upstairs and get my Bible. I'll come back with dinner."

Brian heard her sneakers thump up the stairs, and the storm rattled the window.

He wrapped his hands around Cassandra's. "I'm with you, baby. It's Brian. You stay with me, you hear? Just stay with my voice. If you do, I promise to take you to Aruba when this is done. Palm trees, fruity drinks, walks in the sand, you name it. Just…just stay with me."

CHAPTER TWENTY-FOUR

Brian forced himself to eat some sausage and peppers, along with a side of pasta and a salad. He noticed Alice tuck more into her dinner, too. They were both preparing.

The news said the hurricane was expected to hit the Bronx in an hour. It was almost nine o'clock. They had spent the entire day waiting for two forces of nature; one outside, and one inside.

Howling winds shook the house. So much rain had already fallen, the unfinished basement was beginning to flood. That was the least of his concerns.

At one point, the blinds shook, making him go rigid with anticipation.

"It could be the wind," Alice said, her finger keeping her place in her leather-bound Bible.

"Yeah, it could be."

The local meteorologist was about to tell them when the storm would pass when the TV winked out. A sharp crack hit the shingles outside.

Brian pulled the blinds back to look, but it was too dark, the rain smearing the window, distorting the view. "Well, there goes the cable line. Wind must have snapped it off."

Alice turned the knob on the battery-powered radio she'd brought into the room. The news blared to life.

"I prefer the radio, anyway," she said.

The storm shrieked and the house shook like it was caught in a minor earthquake. Brian watched the IV pole shimmy with the vibration. "You're missing a heck of a storm," he said to Cassandra. "I know how much you love the rain, especially at night, but this one's off the charts. I really wish you'd open your eyes so you can see it, too."

He kept urging her to wake up, to join them as they sat out the storm. Maybe something would get through to her.

Rain pelted the window with renewed fury.

A picture frame fell from the wall. Alice jumped from her chair, the Bible slapping on the floor.

"That picture was hung with two screws," she said, biting back panic.

Brian bent to pick it up, the glass cracked over his and Cassandra's smiling faces.

The room went dark.

Cassandra's life support machine beeped once, more of a high-pitched scream. Then it quieted down as it switched to the battery power.

Alice snapped on the palm-sized flashlight she'd kept looped around her wrist.

"The storm?" she said.

Brian looked out the window again. He saw lights on in Bill/Bob's house. Other houses in back of them also had their lights.

"Just us." His stomach clenched.

Alice lit a candle on the night table.

She shrieked when the infusion pump screeched again, this time fading out as the displays went blank. The radio tuned out as well, the volume getting lower and lower until it too was dead.

"He's coming," Alice said in a trembling whisper.

Brian could feel it too, like a rush of air that precedes an oncoming train.

"I have to turn the generator on. Stay with Cass, keep talking to her. I'll be right back."

He stepped over the cable he'd run from the generator to the life support machine, grabbed the handle to the door and steadied himself.

Be ready for anything on the other side of that door.

He jerked it open and was relieved to see a dark, empty hallway. He flicked on his flashlight and ran to the basement. He could hear Alice reading to Cassandra from the Bible.

The water was an inch high in the basement. He'd put the generator on a makeshift table made of old cinderblocks by a louver ventilation window. His finger hit the ON button and nothing happened. He tried it again. Still nothing.

Flipping through the manual he kept by the generator, he went through the setup guide to make sure he didn't do something wrong. But it had worked just fine when he'd tested it this morning.

With terrible clarity, he realized the generator wouldn't turn on, no matter what he did.

Then Alice screamed.

CHAPTER TWENTY-FIVE

Brian ran up the stairs and rushed back to the bedroom. Several candles had been lit. Alice stood apart from the bed, her eyes wide, terrified, arms locked at her sides.

The cream-colored sheet they had draped over Cassandra was slowly pulled toward the foot of the bed. Invisible fingers gathered the material, balling it into a tight bunch as Cass's atrophied body was revealed inch by inch.

Time stopped for Brian. He could no longer hear the storm crashing around the house or Alice's helpless cries.

He watched as the sheet slipped over Cassandra's exposed knees. Her pale flesh broke out in goose bumps. She may have been unconscious, but somehow he knew she could feel the violation of her personal space by the unseen hands.

He gasped when he looked to her face and saw her hair parting along her pillow, as if someone or some*thing* was stroking it.

Alice's voice cut through the numbness. "Brian, make it stop."

Yes! Do something! Take her from it!

Brian shook his head, breaking the dull haze that enveloped his brain. He reached down to pull Cassandra to him.

The icy barrier chilled him to his bones. It felt as if Cassandra was immersed in the center of a glacier. The cold was so extreme, it burned.

Stifling back a cry, he covered her as much as he could with his own body.

She trembled beneath him, and at first he thought it was the hurricane shuddering the house again. When he glanced at her face, he saw foam dripping from her anemic lips. Her tremors escalated until she convulsed in a full-on seizure.

"Cass! Cass!" Brian screamed.

Alice held down Cassandra's legs while Brian kept her shoulders on the bed. The seizure, though violent, was short-lived. Her mouth hung slack while white, frothy bubbles flowed freely. He wiped them away with a corner of a pillowcase.

"I'm calling 9-1-1," Alice said, fumbling for her cell phone.

"They won't come out in this storm."

"I don't care. We need help."

A shock ran through him when he placed his hand on Cassandra's chest.

She's not breathing!

Brian placed a hand behind her neck and tilted her chin up. He bent an index finger and scooped it along the inside of her mouth.

"Brian, what's wrong?"

"She's not breathing," he replied, panic building in his chest. He probed with his finger. "She didn't swallow her tongue and nothing's lodged in her throat that I can see."

Cupping his hands together, he started giving her chest compressions. Alice stood beside him, weeping now, waiting for 9-1-1 dispatch to answer the line.

Another roar from the hurricane slammed the house.

Outside the bedroom door, they heard the slow, steady approach of footsteps.

The boy, his face thrown into deathly shadows by the flickering candlelight, walked into the room.

Alice dropped her phone and staggered back against the far wall. Her mouth hung open, locked in a silent scream.

Brian turned to face the boy, James Thomas, and shouted, "No! You can't have her! She's not yours to take!"

He continued with the chest compressions, his eyes darting between Cassandra and the boy who stood beside the bed, waiting.

Louisa's voice echoed in his head.

He wants Cassandra. Right now, she's in a place that's not quite life, not quite death. It's a place where the bhoot *can grab hold of her. She's in his domain.*

The boy walked closer, reaching out with a tiny hand to touch her. "Mommy."

The words were clear, but his lips didn't move.

"No! She's not your mother!" Brian screamed. "Come on, baby, come back to me." His voice quivered with desperation. His arms ached and tears stung his eyes.

One-one thousand, two-one thousand, three-one thousand, push!

Cassandra's body suddenly arced beneath him, and she gasped for air.

"Mommy?"

Brian struggled to get his weight off her chest and stomach.

The boy watched him with cold eyes from the other side of the bed.

Cassandra's eyes fluttered open. Brian pulled her body to the far end of the bed, away from the boy. He wrapped his arms around her chest, grateful to feel it rise and fall. Her skin was cold and clammy, but she was awake and alive.

Alice stood frozen in her fear, behind the bhoot.

When he kissed Cassandra's cold lips, she struggled to say, "B-Brian?" His name came out in a dry, pained rasp.

"Yes, Cass, it's me. Did you hear me calling for you?"

Her eyes rolled and her head turned to the boy. His face had gone slack, emotionless. She turned back to Brian, confused. She whispered, "I never want to leave you. I love you."

Brian's body shook with sobs. "I know, honey, I know."

He locked gazes with the boy and felt the contempt, the despair. The door slammed shut, opened and closed again with deliberate, violent force. The floor quaked and the lathing in the ceiling sounded like it was being pulled apart.

The boy reached out to Cassandra. Brian tightened his grip on her, edging her further away from the bhoot's grasp. When Cassandra winced, the boy took a step forward.

"No more hurt, Mommy."

"Don't you touch her!" Alice cried. She threw herself between the boy and her daughter. The boy's head snapped in her direction and she froze, just the tips of the toes on her right foot touching the ground, her arms outstretched. Even her panicked gaze was locked on her face. It was as if she had been frozen in time.

A growling wind shook the foundation of the house. Or was it the frustration of the bhoot? Brian scooted until his back hit the wall. He held tight enough onto Cassandra to hurt her, but she wasn't making a solitary complaint.

"Let her go," Brian commanded the spirit boy.

The bhoot glowered at him, his anger fading when his eyes drifted down to Cassandra.

Shifting Cassandra to his side just enough to block her with his body, Brian reached out to grab Alice's hand. He swiped at empty air, the space between them as cold as the moon. He shifted to get closer, but not so much as he would lose too much contact with his wife. His fingers touched Alice's, curling over them, using them to pull his hand further up her palm. When he had a good grip on her hand, he yanked as hard as he could.

Alice didn't move. He couldn't tell if she was even breathing. Her flesh was sub-arctic; so cold, it was starting to numb his hand.

His eyes flashed to the bhoot. "She didn't do anything to you. You're hurting her, you son of a bitch!"

His words got through to the boy, because in the next instant her hand was ripped from his and she flew backwards across the room.

Alice slammed hard into a padded chair. The wood frame cracked but didn't break. She gasped for breath, as if coming up from deep underwater.

Rain lashed the windows without mercy. Glass exploded as a tree limb javelined into the room. It struck Cassandra's bed and pinwheeled, destroying her life support machine.

Brian felt shards of glass in his face, but he didn't dare take his hands away from Cassandra.

"Why is he doing this?" she sobbed.

It sounded as if the hurricane was going to rip the house apart. The floorboards rattled and the echoes of shattering glass filled the hallways.

The definition of the boy came more and more into focus. He looked back at Alice, as if daring her to stop him, and then turned to Cassandra. Step after slow step, he came closer.

Brian wasn't sure how much Cassandra would be able to comprehend, having just come out of a coma moments ago to pure, incomprehensible chaos. "He...it...he thinks you're his mother."

At the sound of the word mother, the boy said, "*Mommy hurts. I don't want Mommy to hurt. Come stay with me, Mommy. I won't hurt you.*"

The boy's features softened and for a painful moment, Brian felt sorry for the lost, confused soul. Knowing what the boy wanted with Cassandra, he quickly lost sympathy. He whispered in Cassandra's ear, "You have to tell him you're not his mother. I don't think he's going to believe me."

"I'm so scared."

Her body trembled against him even more than the stressed house as it fought against the hurricane.

The boy was just a few short strides away now.

"I know, I know." Brian kissed the side of her face. "I just need you to look him in the eye and tell him the truth."

A whirlwind of leaves blew in through the broken window, filling the room.

The bhoot reached out his hand.

"*Come with me, Mommy.*"

Brian squeezed Cassandra's shoulders. "Tell him now, Cass."

With tears running down her face, Cassandra forced herself to face the both beautiful and terrifying bhoot. "I...I don't know who you are. I'm not...I'm not your mother."

"*Liar!*"

"I know you're scared. I know you want your mommy. But I'm not her."

The boy's eyes blackened and the hair rose from his phantom scalp. "*Come with me now, Mommy!*"

Cassandra stood up faster than Brian could stop her. She looked down at the angry boy, leaves and detritus sticking in her hair as it rode the winds of destruction within the house.

"Look at me," she said, not with anger, but with a tenderness and compassion Brian would not have been able to muster himself. "Your mother isn't here. If I was your mother, I would take you in my arms and hold you forever. You know that, right?"

The cacophony outside and inside the house began to subside. The wind circling in the bedroom calmed, and leaves skittered across the floor. Brian knew the worst of the hurricane had passed just as suddenly as it had started, but he couldn't shake the feeling that the bhoot had some modicum of control of nature itself.

"*Not...Mommy?*"

Cassandra wavered. Brain bolted up to hold her. Her skin was wet and clammy and he could hear the rasping of her lungs. Still, she stood firm, keeping the boy's full attention.

"No, baby. Your mommy isn't here."

The boy looked around the room as if he'd just entered it and was confused by the destruction.

Alice had risen from the chair and had her hands clasped over her chest. Behind her, the billowing curtain settled serenely like a sail that had lost its wind.

"*I want my mommy!*" The boy charged Cassandra.

Brian lifted her and ran from the bhoot's path.

Cassandra screamed, "No! No! No!"

The bhoot's arms missed them, collided with the wall, and then sank into it. The boy's eyes bulged as he stared at the half of his arms not encased in the wall. He turned to Cassandra with a knowing look, a sorrowful acceptance dimming his eyes.

The image of James Thomas began to fade, becoming more ghost-like. His body turned to mist. Only his eyes stayed in sharp focus, clouded with anger, with confusion, and finally, with pained acceptance.

"Your real mommy is waiting for you," Cassandra said.

Suddenly, he broke apart, parts of him reduced to dark shadows fleeing in all directions like a spooked murder of crows flittering around the room until they were absorbed into the walls, floor, and ceiling.

Outside, the brunt of the storm had fully passed, leaving an ear-popping silence in its wake. The electricity returned, bathing Brian, Cassandra, and Alice in soft, white light.

Alice rushed across the room to lock them both in a shaky embrace. She almost knocked them all to the ground as Brian couldn't feel his legs. In fact, he felt numb all over.

Cassandra touched both their faces with cold fingertips and smiled for the first time since their wedding.

The hinges on the door squealed as it opened once again. Brian looked up and saw nothing. Better still, he felt nothing.

He stared into Cassandra's eyes and said, "Welcome back."

CHAPTER TWENTY-SIX

Brian woke up to the sound of birds whistling in the bird feeder Cassandra had hung outside their window. He wasn't crazy about attracting the early risers, but she loved being woken up by their songs.

His arm reached out for her and touched a still-warm, empty side of the bed.

Stretching and yawning, his brain already buzzed with things that needed to be done. He and Cass had been up most of the night talking about plans for her re-birthday. It was the first anniversary of the night of the hurricane, the night she came back to him. She said her re-birthday was just as important as her birthday. Plus, it was a great excuse to get presents twice a year.

He chuckled.

They'd also talked about selling the house and moving somewhere up the line in Westchester County. She thought it was a great idea. It would give them a fresh start. For Brian, the house held too many dark memories of things he wanted to leave far behind. Alice and his parents had been more than generous in their offers of financial assistance to get them back on track. Without them, they would have been in insurmountable debt.

"We should put it on the market soon," she'd said. "Besides, I can't look at that room downstairs without thinking about being sick."

Brian put his robe on and called out, "Hey Cass, do you want pancakes or waffles?"

Shuffling and still yawning, he heard her voice in the other room.

"I just took the test. Yep, I'm pregnant. No, I haven't told him yet."

Brian's heart swelled with the news. *I'm going to be a father!* And this after all of the doctors telling them she'd never be able to conceive. So much for their professional opinions.

This was too much. He couldn't resist breaking in on her phone conversation. Was she talking to her mother? To Marybeth? *I'll bet there's a lot of screaming on the other end.*

When he entered the room, his stomach dropped to the floor.

Cassandra sat in her rocking chair, holding the little plastic pregnancy test.

The boy, James Thomas, stood in a dark corner of the room, every cell of his incorporeal body tuned to Cassandra.

She didn't notice Brian's presence.

"You see. I promised I'd never leave you, James. Come on. Come to Mommy."

The boy moved across the room with preternatural speed. Brian watched in mute horror as he knelt before Cassandra, bent forward and melted into her body like smoke through a screen window.

Brian backed away from the doorway, unable to tear his eyes away from the awful tableau.

Cassandra closed her eyes, smiling, rubbing her belly and humming a lullaby.

"Oh hush thee my baby,
Thy sire was a knight.
Thy mother a lady,
Both lovely and bright.
The woods and the glens from

The towers which we see,
They are all belonging,
Dear baby to thee."

AFTERWORD

For those of you who read my book, *Creature*, I'm pretty sure that story wouldn't have been possible without *The Waiting*. Whereas *Creature* is a look into the real-life horror my wife and I have experienced over the years and what that does to a decades long love, *The Waiting* is the hammer blow of cold reality that slapped us in the face when we first got married.

Back when I was writing for Samhain Publishing (R.I.P.), I had this notion I would tackle the real-life threatening event that almost took my wife away from me during our first year as husband and wife. Yes, she nearly died (several times over) and yes, I brought her home on life support and spent the better part of a year working that damn machine and keeping a job I detested so there wasn't a gap in our medical benefits. In that respect, though rare for a couple of honeymooners, it's not entirely unusual. Life wears steel-tipped boots and likes to kick us when we least expect it.

My wife did have a home nurse who was absolutely wonderful and helped make me an expert home care husband. Tragically, that nurse died very young, catching Legionnaires' Disease after taking a cruise. My wife's doctor, the one who cries in Cassandra's hospital room in the story (as he did in real life one night) also passed away too soon, but not before telling her to screw the odds and get pregnant. She took his word above all the others who said no way, and we have two beautiful daughters to thank for it.

What really made this a story I wanted to put in a book was the cold hard fact that while my wife recovered from her illness, a boy visited us on a regular basis in our new apartment. I saw him first one night while washing the dishes, having to run into her room to stop him from hitting into anything, only to find he had vanished. I saw him again and again over the next year, but kept it to myself for fear of everyone thinking I had cracked up and wasn't fit to care for my wife.

Imagine my surprise when my wife, now on the mend, out of the blue tells me about a little boy who used to come sit in the room with her. When I asked her to describe him, I got goose bumps that I think are still there these twenty-five years later. He was real, at least to us. When she got better, he disappeared.

But he came back again when she fell ill. And then left. And came back when she was hit by another terrible malady. He made his presence known to me, my wife, and our children many times over the years. What was the strangest part of all is that we were never frightened. It was as if he came bearing nothing but calm, loving vibes. Maybe that's exactly what we all needed.

I really wanted to tell our true story, but Samhain didn't publish nonfiction, so *The Waiting* was born. Unlike in real life, I had to give the phantom boy a true meaning, a back story, and I had to find an end. Wanting to honor my wife's nurse, Louisa, was born and the key bearer to the bhoot.

In reality, we didn't know who or what the boy was as he came and went for twenty-six years.

What I didn't have when I initially wrote *The Waiting* was a possible explanation for the ghost boy or a true ending. We were living in the mystery and had given up searching for answers.

I'm pretty sure I have both now.

In 2019, we were preparing to move from the only home our

children had ever known. It was a two-family house owned by a wonderful woman who had been like a grandmother to all of us. One day, when my oldest daughter was downstairs talking to her, out of the blue she mentioned a little neighbor boy who used to play with her sons all the time. She still felt bad over fifty years later because the boy had died in a tragic accident, impaling himself on a pole not far from the house. His age and description were about as close a match as we could hope to get for the little boy who lived with us.

On the day we moved, my wife sat alone in the house and spoke aloud, hoping the boy was close and could hear her. She told him how much he was loved by us and how she appreciated his looking after her so many times over the years. She urged him not to be afraid, that other people would soon move into the house and he would have a new family to keep him company. She cried for a bit and was just getting up to leave when a voice whispered close to her ear, "Goodbye."

I have wondered if he would follow us to our new house, but so far, he has not, even though my wife fought through the kind of illness that would trigger his return in the past.

In a way, that makes me sad.

Because the old house has sat empty ever since we left.

And in that house is a small boy, left alone to roam the halls.

ABOUT THE AUTHOR

Hunter Shea is an author, podcaster and horror-meister who spends too much time obsessing over the question of the reality of cryptids and watching movies. He's written over 30 books, including the bestseller, *The Montauk Monster*, and a rogues gallery of terror tomes like *Creature, We Are Always Watching, Bigfoot in the Bronx, Slash, Misfits, Loch Ness Revenge, Sinister Entity* and the wildly insane *Mail Order Massacres* and *One Size Eats All* trilogies. He's lived with ghosts, hunted for UFOs, and will never stop in the search for the perfect slice of pizza. You can catch him at his irreverent best on his weekly podcast, Final Guys, or Monster Men, which is now celebrating 10 years of horror and laughs. His Video Visions column at CemeteryDance.com is a nostalgic look back at the wonders of the video store in the '80s. Follow him at www.huntershea.com for all the latest shenanigans.

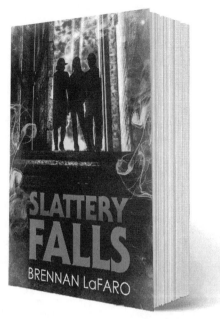

Travis, Elsie, and Josh, college kids with a ghost-hunting habit, scour New England for the most interesting haunted locales. Their journey eventually leads them to Slattery Falls, a small Massachusetts town living in the shadow of the Weeks House. The former home of the town's most sinister and feared resident sits empty. At least that's what the citizens say. It's all in good fun. But after navigating the strange home, they find the residents couldn't be more wrong. And now the roles are reversed. The hunters have become the hunted. Something evil refuses to release its grip, forcing the trio into one last adventure.

Nick has revered his grandfather his entire life. The absent hero, his namesake, buried alive in his final act of courage an ocean and thousands of miles away. Jess has outgrown her status as an all-action social media celebrity and the endless demands that come with it. Adventure Travel TV has thrown this unlikely duo together, promising Jess the launchpad she craves and Nick the chance to tell his grandfather's story first-hand, in the newly uncovered mine that still holds his remains from the twilight days of the gold rush. Is it a dream come true or a nightmare as someone or something stirs...BELOW.

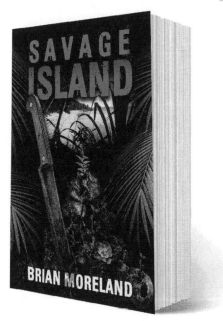

Terror in tropical paradise

On an isolated island in the Philippines, it patiently waits. A mysterious terror lurks in the shadows, stalking the poor stranded souls who visit the island. When a group of four tourists find their vacation quickly turning into a nightmare, the terror taunts them and comes for them one by one. The sandy beach and crystal waters of the lagoon will run red with blood if they can't find a way off this savage island.

Made in the USA
Middletown, DE
26 September 2021